JUST ADD WATER

To those that remember when things weren't so serious, and those that want to have that again.

Just Add Water

ASHLEY GOOD

Chapter One

That was it, the last box. Taylor looked around her empty bedroom. Her *former* bedroom, she reminded herself. The white walls were now bare, save for a few gobs of blue sticky tack that once hung up an assortment of posters. All of her belongings, any sign that she had once lived here, had been packed up into an old leather suitcase set that used to belong to her parents. Or rather, still belonged to them. Taylor's dad had specifically requested that she return them once she unpacked everything in her new room. The only sign that this was once the bedroom of a teenage girl was the sun-bleached outlines of various shapes on an old cedar desk. Taylor told her parents that the desk would look better if the stickers were left on it, but they were adamant that she scrubbed them off before she moved. Sadness washed over her as she double checked all the now vacant dresser drawers. While her parents assured her that she would be able to move back anytime, Taylor knew that this was a guest room now. And that's what she would be if she came back to stay with her parents: a guest.

Not many thirteen-year-old girls had the guts to strike out on their own the way that Taylor was doing, but she certainly didn't feel brave in this moment. She felt like a scared little child who deep down just wanted her parents to hug her and tell her that she didn't need to leave, that she could stay if she wanted to, but that wasn't the kind of relationship they had.

Taylor inspected the walk-in closet one last time. It was clearly empty, but she just wanted to be certain. Not many kids in Craigellachie, British Columbia, had their own walk-in closet and private bathroom, but then again, there weren't many kids in Craigellachie. It wasn't a town per se, or in any sort of say, actually. Craigellachie was a pit stop. No... That's not quite right, either. The region didn't have any gas stations, or amenities that would make it worthy of the title 'pit stop'. Rather, Craigellachie was a location marked by a sign, signifying to travellers that there were in fact houses in this area, they just weren't visible from the highway. A non-place. Oh, there was also a small museum and gift shop which Taylor tended to forget about. Craigellachie was the proud home of the last spike that was placed in the Canadian Pacific Railroad. Train enthusiasts and history buffs that had exhausted all other places of interest could stop and take pictures with a rusty spike, should they choose. Taylor used to wonder why the Chinese workers that built the railroad didn't get more recognition at this historical site. She had asked her parents about it once but they simply brushed off her questions by telling her to "read a book", which was all well and good but the nearest library was a twenty-minute drive away in Sicamous; an almost-place with a population of about 2,000.

"Are you just going to stand here moping all day?" Taylor's mom asked.

Taylor jumped, startled. "Oh, hey. Just making sure I didn't forget to pack something."

"Well get a move on!" Taylor's mom ordered, "Your dad is out waiting in the car. I told Vanessa we would be dropping you off by four, and it's already noon.

Taylor's parents, or Mr. and Mrs. Gagnon, as her friends would have called them, if Taylor had any friends – or Mr. and Mrs. Gagged-On, if Taylor had any bullies – were an older couple in their late fifties. Taylor was an oops baby, or a surprise gift from God, as more polite people might say. After raising their first daughter, Vanessa, until she moved out abruptly at sixteen, the Gagnons decided to move from the genuine-place of Salmon Arm to the non-place of Craigellachie when Taylor was two years old. They were set on retiring somewhere quiet and weren't going to let an unexpected second child stand in the way of that. Besides, they had both been teachers in a past life; they were confident that they could home school Taylor just fine. She could grow up playing in the woods behind the house, fishing in the creek, and swimming in the lake. The perfect childhood. They neglected to think that maybe, just maybe, Taylor would have benefited from interacting with other humans.

It was at the behest of Vanessa, whom Taylor had stayed in touch with over the years, that Taylor was moving to Kelowna to live with her while completing high school. Vanessa had a stable job and wanted to get to know her sister better. During their weekly phone calls, Vanessa would express vague concerns about Taylor growing up "sheltered" or "weird." Taylor knew not to take offence to her sister's words. She was sheltered *and* weird. At least, that's how she felt. Besides, with Taylor gone, her parents could finally live their lives of solitude without an uppity teenager in the house. Taylor was secretly certain that eventually she was going to need counseling because of all of this. At least, that's what she gathered from the few episodes of the new show, Frasier, that she occasionally watched with her parents. Cable TV was a saving grace for a teenager in a non-place in 1994.

Taylor had never thought about how much space she took up or how many belongings she really had. Everything useful in the Gagnon family's home was just *there*. It was as if the furniture came with the house and would remain there indefinitely. She was always asked to keep her personal stuff — books, scrunchies, and in the distant past, toys — in her room. Out of sight out of mind was the Gagnon's parenting model. Taylor was also just *there*. Once all of Taylor's belongings were packed into her parents' beige Oldsmobile Cutlass, she realized how small her existence was.

As Taylor and her parents drove down the Trans Canada Highway, she wondered how life would change living in Kelowna. Would she feel bigger, more confident in a big city? Big was a relative term, she supposed. With roughly 80,000 people, Kelowna was still much smaller than Vancouver, the real big city in the province of British Columbia — Taylor had researched this thoroughly. But deep down she knew that anywhere was going to be better for her than her childhood village of several dozen. As they drove past Eagle River, and eventually Mara Lake, she reminisced about her old pet goldfish that her parents bought her for a biology lesson. How it stayed small, because it was in a small bowl. The tragic nature of how it was only able to grow as large as its surroundings. *I am like a darn goldfish*, Taylor realized.

Taylor's daydreams about life in the big city were interrupted as her dad pulled the boat of a car into the Circle K gas station in Sicamous.

"If you've got to pee, now's your last chance. I don't want to stop again if we can help it," Mr. Gagnon explained while unbuckling his thick grey polyester seat belt.

Taylor followed her dad into the convenience store, while her mom went to use the washroom. A sense of joy washed over her as she looked around at all the overly processed snacks. She often stopped here for snacks after her parents would drop her off at the library which was a block away. Everything was a block away in Sicamous. Taylor picked up a package of Sno Balls and placed them on the counter. The pink coconut and marshmallow covered snacks provided a pop of colour to the grey and oddly sticky gas station counter. Something about prepackaged food felt so metropolitan to Taylor. Her mom always cooked healthy meals at home, so having sugary treats like the kids in commercials felt special.

"Could I get this too, Dad?"

"Ah, why not," Taylor's dad responded lovingly. "I guess since we didn't really throw a going away party, you might as well have a treat now. Actually, go grab a few more packs."

With the car gassed up, bladders emptied, and sugary treats in hand, the Gagnon family was back on the road. Taylor caught her dad's reflection in the driver's mirror and held up the coconut covered confection as if she was toasting. While they didn't always get along, Taylor never doubted that she was loved. It was just complicated, she supposed. Both of her parents raised their Sno Balls and returned the toast.

"To new beginnings!" Mrs. Gagnon cheered.

In that moment, everyone was happy for different reasons. While they tried to hide it, Taylor's parents were excited to restart their retirement, while Taylor was eager to begin her new city life. Only two hours to go!

Slightly less than two hours later, the Gagnon family's car pulled into a parking spot alongside a large brown stuccoed apartment building: The Manhattan Manor. *Wow*, Taylor thought to herself. No, this wasn't actually a manor in New York, but for a homeschooled teenager from a region with about fifty people, this felt like a huge step up in life. Taylor swiftly hopped out of the car. It wasn't just because she was excited – the air-conditioning in the car made her mother feel gross and sticky, so the family had driven for the past two hours with their windows down. It wasn't an issue on the highway but driving through Kelowna at fifty kilometres an hour in August had turned the car into a polyester-lined sauna.

"Sweet Jesus, we're finally here," Mrs. Gagnon muttered to herself, before announcing to the family, "Does anyone know which apartment Vanessa lives in? I really have to pee."

Mr. Gagnon rolled his eyes at his wife's question, while lifting Taylor's tanned leather suitcases out of the trunk of the car. He greatly underestimated how heavy thirteen years' worth of life's belongings could be and strained his back as he lifted with the confidence of a much younger man. Ouch. Now he was going to have to drive the entire way home in pain. Her father knew if he told his wife he pulled his back again for the second time this summer, she would make him see a chiropractor; he just didn't trust that sort of voodoo science.

"Hey, Taylor, come help your old man out and grab these suitcases, will ya?"

"Hun, did you hurt your back again—" Mrs. Gagnon interjected.

"No, my back is fine. I was just thinking that Taylor should have the experience of packing her own stuff into her new apartment. It's a monumental day," Mr. Gagnon excused while passing his daughter the heaviest of the two bags. Taylor carried it with ease, which made Mr. Gagnon think that maybe he should see a chiropractor after all...

Between the three of them, the family managed to carry all of Taylor's belongings to the front of the apartment building in one trip. Taylor stared at the list of names next to the buzzer. Which place belonged to her sister? The list of names jumped from A. Garrison to S. Gladwell. She couldn't see Gagnon listed anywhere.

"That's right, Vanessa is listed under Smith," Mr. Gagnon mused aloud. There it was, the name V. Smith, assigned to buzzer twenty-three, which wasn't attached to an apartment number. "I convinced your sister to use a different name on public things like this for safety reasons. Glad to see she took my advice."

"What do you mean? Why would a fake name be safer?" Taylor questioned.

"The world is full of dangerous people," Mrs. Gagnon answered on behalf of her husband. "You can never be too careful, especially as a single woman."

"Doesn't Vanessa have a girlfrie—" Taylor began.

"—A what?" Her mom interrupted.

"Never mind," Taylor mumbled. She had only been in Kelowna for fifteen minutes and already she was nervous she had said something wrong or betrayed her sister's trust. Her stomach sunk as her mom looked at her oddly.

"Hey, are you Vanessa's family?" A spunky looking woman asked. Taylor looked her up and down. She was dressed in a t-shirt that Taylor figured was a reference to Buddhism, a plaid button-down shirt, and tattered jeans. Her shaggy brown hair made her a dead ringer for Winona Ryder. Taylor wondered if this woman was employed in the forest industry, before realizing that she must be a part of the grunge scene like she had seen on MuchMusic. Maybe this woman was in a band?

Maybe she would take Taylor to concerts? She was so cool. Taylor instantly wanted to be her best friend.

"Hi, yeah, we are. I'm her sister, Taylor."

"It's great to meet you, Taylor. I'm Tara," Taylor's new favourite person replied, offering a confident handshake. "Nes should be on her way home from work. She made plans to leave... Around now, actually," Tara said while checking her watch. "She didn't want you to have to wait outside in case you were early, so she asked me to wait in the lobby to give you guys the keys. Her apartment is on the third floor, unit 315."

"You mean, our daughter is avoiding us again," Mrs. Gagnon retorted, while grabbing the key from Tara before Taylor could. Mr. Gagnon once again caught himself rolling his eyes at his wife.

"Mom..." Taylor groaned while staring at the ground.

"I don't know what to tell you, I'm just the messenger," Tara offered nonchalantly. "She promised to be here by the time you arrived at four, and you're early so... If you wait around in the apartment, I'm sure she'll be here soon. Here, why don't I take one of those bags, and show you guys the way."

After a short elevator ride, possibly the third one that Taylor had ever taken, they arrived at Vanessa's apartment. Taylor stood in front of the door for a moment and traced her fingers around the metal number that was affixed to the heavy wooden door. *Number 315, my first apartment...*

"Scoot please," Mrs. Gagnon ordered as she opened the door as quickly as she could. She stepped into the apartment, kicked off her shoes and turned left, then right, and made a bee line for the washroom. At first Taylor wondered how her mom knew which room was the washroom, but then realized that the apartment wasn't very big.

"Huh, not bad, not bad..." Mr. Gagnon said to no one in particular, as he took in his surroundings. "It's much cleaner than I was expecting... The air-conditioning is also a bonus. But I'm not thrilled about some of this art," he said as he gestured to a wall coated in posters and zines. "Bikini Kill? Jack Off Jill? I hope she doesn't watch or listen to this sort of stuff now that her little sister is moving in."

I hope she does, Taylor thought spitefully.

"But the furniture and everything else looks good. Very modern," Mr. Gagnon said while taking in the clean off-white walls and tightly woven brown carpeting. There was something about an apartment in its original condition that made him happy; he always found painted walls and outward expressions of style to be terribly overrated. He wished that everyone could be as utilitarian as him.

"Welcome to your new home, Taylor," Tara said as she placed her hand on Taylor's shoulder. "I should get going. If you need anything, I'm just down the hall in 319. It was nice to meet you, Mister and Missus Gagged-on," Tara said, as Mrs. Gagnon stepped out of the washroom. Taylor wasn't sure if she had heard Tara correctly.

"We should probably get going too," Taylor's parents both mumbled in a sort of unison, oblivious to Tara's misnaming.

"You're not going to stay and wait to see Vanessa?" Taylor questioned.

"No, it's a two-hour drive back to Craigellachie, and we want to be home for dinner," her dad replied.

"But it's only two now. We got here early."

"Listen to your father, Taylor. This wasn't meant to be a big ordeal, we just agreed to drive you here and drop you off," Taylor's mom said, while putting her shoes back on.

"You're just going to leave me here, alone?"

"You're not alone, I saw a TV in the living room. Plus, you heard that lumberjack woman, she's just down the hall if you need anything. Now come here and give your parents a hug before they leave," Mr. Gagnon said while leaning in to give his daughter a half-hearted squeeze. Mrs. Gagnon wrapped her left arm partially around Taylor as well, resulting in a less than enthusiastic group hug. If an alien looked through the roof of this apartment and witnessed this hug, they would have thought that it was a hostage hand-off situation.

=After the stiff show of affection ended, Mrs. Gagnon passed Taylor the key to the apartment. "Make sure you call us on the weekend," Mr. Gagnon said, before they both left Taylor alone in the apartment. In that moment, Taylor had never felt happier. She could finally exist without her parents breathing down her neck. The air-conditioning was also very refreshing.

Chapter Two

Vanessa, or Nes, as her friends – when she had friends – would call her, was staring into the screen of a block-like IBM computer. The computer sat directly in the middle of Vanessa's pressed fiberboard desk, next to an aged taupe phone, several scattered Post-it Notes covered in atrociously messy handwriting, and a mostly empty tube of Dr. Pepper Lip Smackers that Vanessa kept around just to occasionally smell. She wasn't staring at the computer with intent, it was just where her gaze had wandered. The green cursor bar blinked consistently, representing a series of zeros and ones. Blink, blink, blink, blink... Zero, one, zero, one... On, off, on, off...

Vanessa used to find the idea of computers fascinating; the fact that everything they did was because of commands being implemented by simple zeros and ones, known as binary code, blew her mind. However, she found this particular computer underwhelming. All it was used for was pulling up customer files when they called in to ask questions about their cable con- nection. Most of their questions were the same: *Why doesn't my TV work? Can I sign up for a cable subscription?* And *Can I pay less for my cable subscription?* Up until recently, Vanessa and the rest of the cable support team used a paper filing system which worked just fine. And then abruptly one day last year, right after their small cable company merged with a larger telecommunications company, their boss dropped off one of these grey blocks into everyone's cubicles. It was cool at first to have computers at work – to see one outside of the movies – but once Vanessa and her cynical colleagues all realized that they couldn't use these machines to access some sort of War Games simulation, the novelty wore off.

When Vanessa was first hired for this customer support job ten years prior in 1984, she was excited. Excited because she loved television and was excited to help bring cable into everyone's homes, but also excited because it beat flipping burgers. Vanessa got her first fast food job at an old burger joint along Okanagan Lake as soon as she moved out on her own at sixteen. At sixteen, flipping burgers wasn't that bad. There were certainly worse things that a teenager could do to pay the bills. Vanessa could deal with the long hours on her feet and constantly smelling like onions and used deep fryer oil, but after a few years, she wanted something more stable and better paying. And a job that wouldn't make her dates recoil when they met her for drinks right after work. *Oh, you like my perfume? It's eau de ground beef...* After answering an ad in the classifieds section of the newspaper, Vanessa quickly found herself exchanging her brightly coloured greasy polyester fast-food uniform for a wardrobe of brightly coloured polyester outfits with shoulder pads. Each time she bought a new shirt, she vowed to cut the shoulder pads out, but would inevitably forget before just growing accustomed to the shirt with the foam left in.

After a decade of working this customer support job in years' worth of similarly styled and similarly uncomfortable business clothes, Vanessa's excitement for the job and life in general, had faded. The only thing that consistently brought her joy was attending punk shows on Friday nights with her long-time girlfriend, Tara Smith. Although, her and Tara were both beginning to realize that at twenty-eight and twenty-six-years-old respectively, they were growing out of the scene. One by one their old friends disappeared as they each got their own stuffy jobs. Vanessa struggled to under-stand why they couldn't balance the punk scene with a corporate job the way that she did. Tara often tried to explain to her that perhaps their friends just felt hypocritical about working for "the man" while rallying against the system on weekends, but Vanessa doubted that any of her former friends cared that much about it. They were obviously just boring.

The lack of thrills in her life wasn't something that Vanessa spent too much time contemplating. It was just on her mind today as she was excited for the first time in ages; her little sister, Taylor, was finally coming to live with her and Tara. Vanessa had been trying to convince her parents for the past several years to let Taylor move to Kelowna with her. She knew that they were unhappy with a kid at home, and she felt that she could offer Taylor a much brighter future. Plus, she was saving decent money being a boring adult; she might as well use it to help her kid sister. Taylor was great, too. A little shy, sure, but Vanessa was confident that she would blossom once she was in the city and enrolled in a proper school.

Realizing that she had been staring at the computer unblinkingly for the greater part of an hour, Vanessa rolled around in her chair to the clock that was hanging on the side of her grey cubicle wall. It was 1:30PM. Oops. She was supposed to leave work half an hour ago, as she had several stops before going home to greet her sister and parents later this afternoon. She also felt shameful that she had asked Tara to wait in the lobby in case they were early, and lie about living in another apartment. At this point in her life, she had grown to accept that her parents would never respect her or her "lifestyle," as Mrs. Gagnon smarmily referred to Vanessa's entire existence. Although Vanessa had learned to understand that her parents were rigid in their beliefs, and that their cruelty wasn't her fault or something that she could control, thinking about it was still angering. At least finally, at long last, her little sister was going to be away from those bigots. Vanessa was thrilled to be able to let Taylor have the teenage experience that she herself couldn't have growing up, and she wasn't about to start things off on the wrong foot by being late.

Vanessa grabbed her jacket off the back of her spinning chair and hurried out of the cubicle. She returned quickly to grab one of the messy Post-it Notes:

Groceries: cereal, milk, pizza, and cake! Don't forget!

Chapter Three

According to the clock on the microwave, it was 2:46PM. According to the flashing clock on the oven, though, it was 12:00, so who could really say for certain how accurate the microwave was. Taylor didn't have a watch. Being homeschooled and living according to her parents' schedule, Taylor always relied on them to tell her what to do and when. Now however, she was all alone in this new apartment. While she knew that it wasn't rational, Taylor found herself growing increasingly anxious about the lack of an inaccurate clock. Thankfully she was able to keep herself distracted by exploring the fully stocked kitchen.

Michelle! Why is the dog purple?
Purple? Looks more like violet to me.
Audience laughter.

Uncomfortable with silence, Taylor had turned the TV on to give the apartment some atmosphere. No matter what was happening in her life, sitcoms always brought her comfort. As sheltered as Taylor's upbringing had been so far, even she knew that they were a little cheesy. Speaking of cheese, she was happy to see that her sister had several kinds in the fridge. *Cheddar, cream cheese, and Havarti?* Taylor was relieved that her sister's good taste wasn't just relegated to band posters. And where was her sister, anyway? Tara said that Vanessa would be home soon, but it had already been forty-five minutes. Was her sister always tardy?

I wanted us to match!
Did you ask Cosmo if he wanted to be purple?
Dog barks.
More laughter.

"Hey Taylor!" Vanessa announced as she walked through the front door carrying a stack of boxes, in a coincidentally very sitcom-esque way.

"Oh my God!" Taylor jumped, startled and embarrassed to be caught examining the bottles of blackberry Clearly Canadians at the back of the fridge.

"Relax, I'm not our parents," Vanessa spoke coolly while setting the boxes of pizza and a cake on the counter. "Speaking of which, where are they?"

"Oh, Mom and Dad left after dropping me off. They said they'd come back on the weekend to grab the suitcases, but who knows."

A look washed over Vanessa's face. Taylor wasn't sure if it was sadness or a sense of relief. Maybe both? "Well, it's their loss, I guess," Vanessa reasoned while gesturing towards the food. She suddenly felt even more awful about having asked Tara to stay with a friend until she was certain her parents had left. "I thought we'd celebrate your big move, so I got us pizza – you still like Hawaiian, right? – and this giant sheet cake. They didn't have any with relevant writing and it was going to take another two hours to get something custom, but it all tastes the same."

Taylor looked down at the cake.

Congratulations birthday boy!

It was neither her birthday nor was she a boy, but this was still one of the sweetest gestures that Taylor could recall. Even on her birthday, her parents typically bought cake that they preferred. Their go-to was black forest cake because it was "better." All Taylor ever wanted was some darn confetti cake…

"I think it's a confetti cake," Vanessa said.

That was it: Taylor was now sure that this really was the best day ever. She ran towards her sister and gave her a giant hug, which was easy to do since everyone in their family were lanky with oddly long arms. Hence Taylor's childhood nick-name…

"It's about time! I've missed you, Stringbean."

"I've missed you too."

"You're so much taller than I remember."

"Well, I am thirteen now."

"We've got a lot of catching up to do," Vanessa spoke sincerely. "Now let's dig into this food before we start unpacking your room. I know Dad hates to stop for food when he's driving, so you're probably starving!"

Taylor grabbed a plate from the cupboard. It was thin and white with little brown flowers etched along the rim. She loaded up the plate with greasy ham and pineapple pizza. The heat from the pizza radiated through the thin plate and warmed her hands as she walked back to the living room.

Wait, why does the dog smell like grape?

I dyed him with Kool-Aid!

Uproarious laughter!

"Hey Nes… After we unpack, could we go to the mall so I can get a watch?"

"Whatever you want to do, Stringbean—" Vanessa said with a smile, while grabbing the TV remote from the coffee table, "—except watch this show." She clicked through channels until she ended up on some sort of show with a professional-looking woman sitting on a couch. Taylor wasn't sure what the show was about, but it felt very serious and adult.

A wave of insecurity washed over Taylor. She should have known that someone as cool as her adult sister wouldn't want to watch a silly sitcom. Without having said anything, it became clear that her mood had shifted.

"I'm sorry Taylor, I wasn't implying you had bad taste. Sitcoms, or rather, family shows in general, just aren't my thing. Although I do think that Alanis and Dave Coulier make a cute couple. Anyway, you can and should like whatever you want! Don't let anyone tell you otherwise."

"Mom and Dad never let me pick the shows at home... They put a TV in my room a few birthdays ago, though."

"Wow, they let you put a TV in your room?"

"I think they just wanted me to stay in my room more..."

Vanessa set her pizza down and turned towards her little sister. "When I was your age, I thought that there was something wrong with me. That I would never be happy. Mom and I used to scream all the time – I'm not sure if you remember any of that – but literally every little thing was a battle. Clothes, make-up, school. I used to think I was a broken person because I just couldn't make them happy." Vanessa took a deep breath and considered her next words carefully. "It took me until I was in my mid-twenties, and several counsellor sessions to realize—"

Just like Frasier! Taylor thought.

"—our parents just suck."

It was as if those words were a secret password needed to unlock the next stage of Taylor's life. *Our parents do suck,* Taylor silently agreed. For the first time in her life, she felt validated. The touching moment between the two sisters was abruptly interrupted by a loud commercial.

Hey kids! Are you lonely? Do people find you repulsive? Wouldn't it be easier if you could just buy a friend? Then GROW A FRIEND is the hot new toy for you! For only $24.99 and a splash of water, you can grow your new best friend, human or otherwise!

"Ugh, they've been playing these ads nonstop. And why do commercials always have to be so loud?" Vanessa asked rhetorically with an eye roll.

"Wait, are those real?" Taylor asked hesitantly.

"What do you mean?"

"There's a toy that comes to life?"

"No way. Grow a Friends are just a way to rip off dumb kids who have more money than sense," Vanessa said while lifting up a piece of pizza.

"So, it doesn't really come to life?" Taylor asked with a raised brow.

"I mean, I haven't seen one myself, since they're not out until Christmas, but no, a toy won't just come to life. It's probably just this dinky little toy that flops around or something," Vanessa said while gesturing with her pizza. Mid gesture, Vanessa playfully flicked a piece of pineapple off of her pizza, hitting Taylor square on the cheek.

"Did you really just flick pineapple at me?" Taylor said as she wiped the greasy smear off of her cheek. She then flung her own piece of pineapple, which landed in Vanessa's long permed ash blonde ponytail, like a fruit shaped barrette. They both erupted with laughter.

"I'm glad you're here, Tay," Vanessa said with a smile, while popping the pineapple into her mouth. "Now, let's have some of that cake."

Chapter Four

"Yet another corporate monstrosity…" Tara mumbled, stepping out of the driver's side of her '79 Ford Ranger and gazing up at the new Eaton's department store, attached to the Orchard Park Mall. Big Blue, as she called the truck, was Tara's first vehicle, and if she had her way, would be her only vehicle. She loved her beast of a truck, peeling paint and all. Tara bought the truck used for about five hundred dollars, right around the time Vanessa asked her to move in, which gave it some sentimentality. The truck had seen better days, but Tara was determined to fix it up when she finally got some extra money; with the extra hours she had been picking up at work, she hoped to have enough by next year. Baristas didn't make that much, but thankfully rent was cheap. Vanessa slid across the patchy tweed seats and hopped down onto the hot pavement. Taylor, who had been squished uncomfortably in the middle seat, followed her big sister out of the truck.

"I really wish you'd consider getting a vehicle with backseats," Vanessa called over to Tara, while slamming the truck's much too heavy door. "And air-conditioning."

"Big Blue's got character. Which is more than can be said about most things nowadays..." Tara trailed off again, while staring at the Eaton's store that had been recently added to the mall.

"Is she okay?" Taylor whispered to Vanessa.

"She's fine. She just gets like this every time we go shopping," Vanessa said with an eye roll.

"I'm calling it now: in the future, everything will be a big corporate chain."

"Yes, yes, capitalism is bad. We know Tara," Vanessa jokingly mocked. "The store has been here a year now, though. I don't think it's going anywhere." She looked around subtly before tenderly taking Tara's hand. "My kid sister needs some new clothes, so let's stop with the ranting for now, and have a good time, okay?"

"Fine," Tara responded in a faux-exasperated tone. "But if the kiddo wants anything Disney, I'm out."

Unsure of how to respond, Taylor just shrugged. She wasn't used to being around people, let alone sarcastic ones. That was something she was going to have to get comfortable with.

"So, what type of clothes do you like?" Vanessa asked Taylor as they stepped between the mall's automatic doors. The wall of cold air-conditioned air hit them all at once, like stepping through a portal.

"I don't know, I usually just wear what Mom and Dad buy me..." Taylor spoke, as she looked down at what she was wearing. Jeans, sneakers, and a t-shirt with a howling wolf.

"Yeah, I didn't really peg you for a tourist-booth t-shirt type of girl," Tara put forth.

"I guess I just want to fit in with the other kids at school," Taylor said earnestly, looking to Tara.

"Fit in, stand out... Now that you're finally free from our parents, I just want you to be yourself," Vanessa said while looking through her wallet. "Or rather, to be as much of yourself as you can be for two hundred dollars," she continued, while passing Taylor several folded bills.

"I don't know if I can accept this." Taylor had never held so much cash before. *Two hundred dollars? Am I supposed to dress in jewels?*

"Relax, it's alright. I have a decent job. Let me treat my kid sister, will you?" Vanessa spoke warmly.

"We're childless lesbians. If we didn't spoil you, we'd probably just end up adopting a ton of cats," Tara retorted in her typical sarcastic yet friendly tone. As if right on cue, an older woman walked by and scoffed. Tara and Vanessa let go of each other's hands. "Every time..." Tara muttered.

"What was she mad about? Do you know her?" Taylor asked.

"It's just something that's happened before. Don't worry about it," Vanessa added comfortingly, before leaning forward and messing up her little sister's hair.

"I think I might be getting too old for that," Taylor muttered while fixing the part in her long dirty blonde hair.

"Sorry Stringbean. Hey, why don't you go ahead and check out some stores? We'll meet you in the food court in an hour."

"I still need a watch—"

Before Taylor could finish her sentence, Tara took off her grey plastic Timex watch and passed it to her. "Here, you can use this until you buy your own."

Vanessa leaned towards Taylor and whispered, "She bought that at Eaton's."

Cash tucked in the back pocket of her ill-fitting jeans; Taylor stood alone in the hallway of the Orchard Park Mall. She looked down the expansive hallways at the cross section of the mall's entrance. Large planters full of tropical plants divided the halls into lanes and the sand-coloured floor twinkled slightly as beams of sun crept in from the sky lights. It was oddly pretty, like a manufactured beach, sans water. The other shoppers hurrying around in their brightly hued clothes made Taylor think of the neon fish her parents used to keep in their living room aquarium before they all went belly up, presumably out of boredom.

Suddenly, a wave of panic washed over her. She wished that her sister and Tara would help her shop but she was too embarrassed to ask for help. They trusted her to go shopping on her own, and she didn't want to let them down. She should know how to dress. What stores were "cool" and which ones weren't. Taylor looked down at her worn sneakers. Were they cool? What did cool even really mean? She could feel her chest tighten as her anxiety about shopping turned into a spiral of existential angst. Taking in a deep breath, Taylor reminded herself that she needed this. Just like a goldfish, she needed a new environment, this bigger space, to grow.

It was the afternoon on a hot summer day, which meant that the mall was mostly populated with moms with strollers or seniors walking laps. Taylor was grateful that there weren't any kids her age around. Taking a deep breath of the recirculated mall air, which smelled strongly of cinnamon buns, she realized she could hear Ace of Base's "I Saw the Sign" faintly coming from one of the store's speakers. *That is as good of a sign as any*, Taylor thought, embarrassing herself with her own internal pun.

As she walked towards her targeted store, the song flowed awkwardly with the rest of the Muzak being pumped into the mall. *I saw the sign – Ugh, push it! Push it! – I opened up my eyes, I saw the sign! – Can you feeeel, the loveee, tonighttt...* Eager to escape the musical milkshake that was flooding her ears, she breathed a sigh of relief when she was finally in the store and could only hear a single song. By now, the Ace of Base track had ended, and was replaced with another pop track. Someone asking about what love was? Whoever made this store's mixtape clearly liked Europop. Unsure of what clothes to buy, Taylor stared at a wall that was covered floor to ceiling in stacks of jeans.

"Hey, can I like, help you find anything?" A shy looking young girl asked, her words muffled ever so slightly by her long black hair that was hanging in her face. Taylor looked at the plastic name tag that was pinned to the girl's black t-shirt: Mischa.

"I don't know… I just moved here, and I guess I need new clothes so I look less like an alien," Taylor said while awkwardly trying to make eye contact with Mischa, whose eyes were mostly concealed by long black bangs. Taylor's dad always preached that eye contact and a firm handshake were two of the most important things in life. Also, something about keeping your elbows off tables… Although that part felt less important in this moment.

Mischa looked Taylor up and down. "I like your shoes, they're cool," she mumbled while fidgeting with her multitude of neon coloured jelly bracelets.

Oh, thank God, Taylor thought to herself. *I'm not a complete disaster.* "I like your bracelets," she offered.

"Thanks. Can I show you some shirts though? We've got like, a sale on…" Mischa said as she began to shuffle to the other side of the store. Taylor realized she should follow along. "These ones are pretty good. Plus, they're only like five dollars. So that's cool," Mischa murmured, while presumptuously passing Taylor several shirts off the rack.

"Uh, thank you. These look great," Taylor spoke softly, trying to mimic Mischa's tone and lessen her earlier intense eye contact. "Can I ask, how old are you?"

"Thirteen, but I'm turning fourteen in a few months," Mischa answered. "If you're wondering how I got the job here, my dad had to sign a permission slip thing. It wasn't a big deal…"

"No, I'm just curious. I don't really know anyone here. I just moved here from Craigellachie—"

Mischa stared blankly.

"It's a place in the Shuswap, just passed Sicamous."

"Oh! Sweet. My grandparents live out there," Mischa offered, while continuing to hide behind her bangs.

Relieved to have met someone that had even a remote idea of where she was from, a smile washed over Taylor's face. "Anyway, I just moved here. I'm starting grade eight at K.S.S. in a few weeks. Are you going to go there too?"

"I am. It sucks though. At least, that's what my big bro says," Mischa said with an eye roll. "But you seem cool, so I guess it'll suck less now?" She said more empathetically, realizing that maybe her parents and boss were right, and maybe she was a little rude sometimes. She didn't mean to be though.

"Awesome, I guess I'll see you there?" Taylor said, as she reached into her back pocket for the cash that her sister had given her. Somehow through their short conversation, Mischa had loaded up Taylor with a stack of shirts, which were now being rung up at the cash register.

"Sounds good. That will be fifty-five dollars and twenty-six cents," Mischa stated while bagging up the rest of the shirts.

Taylor left the store excited to have possibly made a friend, and also impressed at how a girl her age just managed to sell her half of a rack of shirts without even asking what her size was.

Looking at the watch that Tara had lent her, Taylor realized that there was still some time to kill. Walking down the center of the mall, past rows of similarly styled clothing stores, acne medication vendors, and a CD store with intimidatingly stylish looking staff, Taylor decided to check out one store in particular: San Francisco Gifts. She vaguely recalled visiting the store as a child; the rows of silly gifts, and how her mom raced to cover Taylor's eyes when she accidentally walked through the beaded curtains and into the back of the store. Now that Taylor was alone, and had her own spending money, she figured that now was as good of a time as any to finally see what was in the back of the store.

Mustering up her confidence, Taylor walked, head held high, past shelves of snow globes and rude t-shirts, and towards the back of San Francisco Gifts. She was a young woman on a mission! Just as she extended her arm to push the seventies-esque beaded curtain out of the way, Taylor found herself stopped by the booming-yet-sardonic voice of the previously unnoticed salesclerk: "It's just adult toys and lava lamps back there."

Taylor spun around and came face to face with the clerk, a forty-something man in a polo shirt, with a bright San Francisco Gifts lanyard hanging around his neck. "Oh! I, uh, I'm sorry," Taylor stammered as her cheeks began to go red.

"Nothing to apologize for. You looked really focused so I didn't want to interrupt you, but I thought you should know what you were about to find," the clerk explained empathetically. "I've got kids your age."

Taylor knew the clerk meant well but couldn't help but be annoyed by him. Determined to be viewed as an independent woman who knew what she wanted and definitely wasn't overwhelmed by the entire shopping experience, Taylor approached the spinner full of watches by the cash register. "Actually, I was looking for these..." she spoke while looking at a bright pink one hanging from the carousel. As the clerk struggled to unhook the security lock from the stack of watches, Taylor spotted an advertisement for the new Grow a Friend toys taped to the interior of the glass countertop. *"Need a friend? Grow a friend!"* the ad proclaimed. She found herself absentmindedly tracing her fingers around the letters on the ad, as the salesclerk finally got the watch off the rack.

Noticing Taylor's interest in the ad, the clerk looked around and leaned towards her discretely. "Hey, so, I probably shouldn't tell you this, but... Our Grow a Friend shipment came early. My boss would be furious if he knew I was trying to sell them before the holidays, but you look like you could, well, use a friend."

"Thanks?" Taylor replied while raising one of her bushy blonde eyebrows, unsure if she should be offended or not.

Reaching into an unmarked cardboard box just below the cash register, the clerk retrieved a Grow a Friend in partially opened packaging. "I accidentally hit this guy with the box cutter when I was opening the container. The toy's mostly fine. Except his sword detached, and the package is a little mangled. It's yours for half off if you want it."

Taylor looked down at the packaging of the Grow a Friend toy. It was in a clear plastic egg, like something that you could get for a buck out of a vending machine. Taylor held the semiopaque plastic egg up to her eyes and peered through the section that had been scratched by the box cutter. Although the Grow a Friend toys came in a variety of possible shapes, this one looked like a tiny fairy-tale prince. He even had a little sponge sword, which was formerly attached to his hand. There was no way this tiny inch long toy was going to come to life in water, but Taylor was intrigued. "Do you have any of the other shapes? What about the dinosaur ones?"

"I do, but not for this price."

She thought about the money her sister had given her, and how it was meant for clothing. The idea of having what was going to be this Christmas' most popular toy several months before everyone else though, was too good of an opportunity to pass up. Her future classmates would be so jealous of her!

"Okay, I'll take it."

The salesclerk bagged up the watch, and Taylor's new Grow a Friend. She paid cash and left the store with a sense of excitement in her stomach. Thinking back to Vanessa and Tara's earlier comments about sitcoms and Disney though, Taylor took the plastic egg out of the San Francisco Gifts bag and tucked it underneath her stack of new shirts. Grow a Friend concealed, Taylor went to meet her sister in the food court.

Chapter Five

Taylor stared at the outfits that were laid out across her bed. A long-sleeved black t-shirt was matched with pre-tattered black jeans, a pink velvet sweater was paired with a pair of red denim pants, and a baggy blue plaid shirt was matched up with a pair of high waisted shorts. Each outfit looked like it belonged to a different person. "I have no idea what I am doing," Taylor muttered to herself as she examined the pink velvet sweater.

Swapping the pink sweater for the blue plaid shirt, she held the shirt against her chest and looked at herself in the sticker-adorned bedroom mirror. It had now been two weeks since Taylor had moved to Kelowna, and she was just as confused and lost feeling as when she had first arrived. She had new clothes, a new bedroom that she was finally allowed to paint bright purple, and was just about to start high school. And yet, Taylor felt like the same old awkward thirteen-year-old.

"Knock knock…" Vanessa called out as she slowly opened her little sister's bedroom door. "Are you doing okay in here?"

"No!" Taylor sighed before dramatically collapsing on her bed.

"The first day of school is stressful, I get it. What specifically is bugging you though?" Vanessa pressed.

"I don't know who I am," Taylor bluntly stated.

"Why, you're Taylor Elizabeth Gagnon, and you're a badass!" Vanessa declared while carefully holding up her hot mug of coffee in a cheer.

Taylor looked down at her feet. "That's not what I meant."

"I know, but we've only got about half an hour before you need to get to school and I need to start work. I'm not sure we have the time for a full-blown identity crisis right now," Vanessa said, before gesturing to the blue plaid shirt that was laid out on the bed. "Blue looks good on you, wear that. And the black jeans."

Sensing her sister was still lost in thought, Vanessa knelt in front of Taylor while balancing her coffee on her right knee. "It's your first day of high school. You have your entire life ahead of you to figure out who you are. Just wear what makes you happy. You've got this."

Just as Taylor was realizing that her sister hadn't concluded her pep talk by messing up her hair, as she would normally do, Vanessa's non-coffee holding hand swooped over Taylor's face and messed up her hair. She rolled her eyes, as she felt silly for not dodging her sister's hand. "Come on, I'm your big sister. I have to do stuff like this," Vanessa said with a smile before leaving Taylor's bedroom.

Taylor stood up and looked at herself in her mirror again. She fixed her hair, before taking her sister's advice and putting on the blue plaid shirt and black tattered pants. The black pants gave off Gwen Stefani-vibes, which was Taylor's goal. She had become a tad obsessed with Gwen Stefani and her band No Doubt, following a rant about "good music" that Tara went on when Taylor casually mentioned liking a song by another woman-led band, Hole. Tara was extremely adamant that the singer in Hole had killed her husband, Kurt Cobain. Taylor had heard of him before, but it was only during Tara's rant that she realized the impact he had on music, and apparently on Tara. Anyway, it was during that rant about listening to rockers that aren't probably murderers that led Taylor to discovering No Doubt. Needless to say, the clerks at Sam's Records were very confused when Taylor told them her non-murderer caveat when looking for new music suggestions. She gave herself a nod of approval in the mirror, before picking her new denim backpack up off the floor and hurrying out of the apartment.

"No, don't worry about me. I've just been waiting here all alone for twenty minutes," Mischa mumbled accusatorily as Taylor approached her in the off-white lobby of the Manhattan Manor.

"I couldn't figure out what to wear. You look great though," Taylor said. She really did like Mischa's all black attire, even though Taylor didn't quite understand the purpose of the goth aesthetic.

"If my dad asks, I wore these," Mischa said sardonically while revealing the vibrant non-goth clothes that were stashed in her safety-pin-covered black nylon backpack. "He insists I wear more colour so it doesn't look like I'm a ghoul or something, so I changed in the 7-Eleven bathroom on my way here."

Mischa, as it turned out, lived in another apartment complex down the road from Taylor. The two of them decided to hang out when Taylor needed to exchange all the clothes that she had purchased two weeks earlier. Usually, Taylor would be annoyed with herself for foolishly not trying on the clothes first and wasting everyone's time by needing to go back to the mall to exchange them, but she was happy she had made a friend. Her first friend.

Living with a single father and older brother had made Mischa extra appreciative that Taylor didn't make frequent fart jokes and enjoyed talking about the boys in magazines without gagging every time Mischa bought a Tiger Beat magazine. Although if anyone else asked, the magazines were for Mischa's fictional little sister. Having a crush on boy banders didn't exactly match the dark and serious public persona she was going for now that she was officially a teenager.

Even though she was going through a totally-not-a-phase goth stage, and more sarcastic than Taylor was used to, Mischa was great to be around. She was fun to hang out with and, although Taylor would never say it out loud, she was also probably a little psychic. If a weird person walked by, or someone said something dumb, Mischa would be the first person to say exactly what everyone was thinking. Taylor liked that about her.

"So… Are you nervous at all?" Mischa asked, doing her best to look Taylor in the eyes, as she opened the front door of the apartment building.

"About starting high school?"

"Yeah, starting school, meeting new people, boys… I know you're from a small town, so it's okay if you're nervous," Mischa spoke as the glass door slowly closed behind them.

"Honestly, now that I've picked out my clothes, I'm not as stressed out as I thought I'd be. I guess I'm just eager to rip the Band-Aid off and get my first day over with," Taylor surprised herself with her revelation. Did she really mean that? Although it was happening slower than she would have liked, Taylor had several moments over the past few weeks that made her realize that she was in fact, growing up.

"Because, it's like, okay if you are nervous. High school is a big deal, and I've heard that there are lot of mean girls and just… if you're nervous, I promise I won't ditch you in the halls," Mischa offered while looking back at the ground as she walked. Tiny flecks of black nail polish fell to the ground as she nervously picked at her nail polish.

In that moment, Taylor saw past Mischa's tough exterior and understood that she was just as insecure, as uncertain, as Taylor was. "I won't ditch you in the halls either, Mischa."

"Thank you," Mischa spoke sincerely, while now fidgeting with the straps on her oversized backpack. Even though it was new – Taylor was with Mischa when she bought it the previous week – the backpack already looked worn and aged. While she'd never openly admit to caring about how things looked, Mischa was proud that she was able to give her backpack a punk edge by using nothing more than sandpaper and safety pins.

Taylor did her best to take in her surroundings as she continued her walk to school. The leaves on the maple trees that lined Leon Avenue and the intersecting Richter Street had all began to turn vibrant hues of orange and red. Although it made her feel silly and vain, the changes of the season made Taylor excited to be able to wear things from her brand-new winter wardrobe. Her parents always told her that things like fashion were frivolous, and that only "idiot city slickers" cared about such things. For the first time in her young life, Taylor was finally in an environment where it felt okay to be herself. It was scary to be starting high school, but Taylor was enjoying these moments of excitement that seemed to happen more and more since she had moved to the city.

There was no commute, no morning walk to school, as a homeschooler in Craigellachie. There was no reason to wear cute outfits, or to meet a friend in the morning. Taylor would wake up, pour a bowl of whatever bland cereal her parents bought in an attempt to be healthy, throw on jeans and a t-shirt, and then work on her monotonous classwork until dinner time. *Maybe the cereal makers thought that if their product tasted bad enough, no one would eat more than a few calories' worth, ipso facto, they could market it as "healthy?"* If she hadn't jumped at the chance to move in with Vanessa, Taylor's life would have been the same everyday until she turned eighteen and finally moved out...

"You okay?" Mischa asked.

"What? Oh, sorry. I'm just being a space case," Taylor said as she looked both ways and began to cross Harvey Avenue with Mischa. She didn't realize that she had been lost in thought for most of their walk.

"I'd rather my new friend *not* get hit by a car," Mischa offered with slightly more sincerity than usual. While she acted like she didn't hear it, because she didn't want to come across as needy, Taylor took the words "new friend" to heart and smiled.

As they crossed the highway, the size of the building that was 575 Harvey Avenue really hit Taylor. While only two floors tall, the behemoth of a high school's expansive red brick walls sprawled out in multiple directions; its multiple hallway wings were like a giant beached octopus. The parking lot was full of countless cars, with a clear divide between the older cars in the student parking side and the newer cars parked on the teachers' side. Overly bass-y music blared from several of the students' cars, as teens laughed, smoked, and flirted. The building itself could easily hold the entire population of Craigellachie, at least ten times over. *Kelowna Secondary School is most definitely a Place,* Taylor thought to herself.

"K.S.S. is like something out of the movies," Taylor whispered to Mischa.

"Haven't you been here before?" Mischa asked, "You live like, three blocks away."

"I wanted my first day to feel special," Taylor confessed.

"Yeah… Probably don't say stuff like that out loud today," Mischa mumbled, while stopping to fix her hair in the reflection of one of the school's windows, her reflection distorted by a summer's worth of dust and smudges. On the other side of the glass, an older teacher watched awkwardly from their desk. Not wanting to lose face, Mischa pretended not to care that the teacher was there, but truthfully, she hadn't noticed them until it was too late. Already committed to what she was doing, and not wanting to run away in embarrassment, Mischa took a small tube of Dr. Pepper Lip Smackers out of her backpack and proceeded to put it on while still using the classroom window as a mirror. The teacher walked over and closed the blinds.

"Joke's on them, the window works better as a mirror this way…" Mischa trailed off, while popping the cap back on the tube of lip balm and trying to play off the entire incident as deliberate. Taylor paused and wondered if she should care more about her appearance, but Mischa quickly squashed her concerns. "You look great, stop worrying."

"Thank you," Taylor spoke, as they approached Kelowna Secondary School's front entrance. Its heavy doors swung open and closed as students constantly flooded in and out. There were nerds, goths, ravers, preps… The flow of students was never ending. To go from being homeschooled to attending the largest high school in the Okanagan Valley was like jumping into the deep end of the pool. Taylor couldn't understand how so many people could live in one town, let alone all go to the same high school. Most of them looked so much older than her too. She looked down at her clothes and instantly felt insecure.

"Don't let them get to you," Mischa offered, almost psychically. "I went to elementary school with most of these people. They're just kids like us. Don't let them get to you, even if they're super stylish…" Mischa really was the embodiment of the fake it until you make it mentality. Even though she was a thirteen-year-old goth girl, Taylor could see Mischa turning into a power-dressing businessperson. She reminded her of Ricki Lake, if Ricki Lake had disdain for her audience and a fear of the camera.

Taylor looked down at her hot pink digital watch. There were only ten minutes until they had to get to homeroom. Homeroom was where they would get their locker numbers as well as their schedules for the semester. Being in eighth grade, the students only got to pick between Art Class and Band Class, so their schedules would all end up being pretty much the same, but Taylor was incredibly excited for her locker. That's when all of this would start to feel real!

While still standing on the steps of the front entrance, both girls turned in unison and looked at each other nervously.

"Let's do this?" Mischa offered. Taylor nodded. The two awkward friends adjusted their clothes and backpacks, and boldly walked through the front doors of their new high school.

Chapter Six

It wouldn't be fair to call Taylor's homeroom a class, for no learning was to ever happen in this room. Each student's locker number, schedule, and important dates for the year was printed on continuous stationary paper which had been haphazardly prepared and placed at each empty desk. Some sheets had tear-away holes on the side, while others did not. Typos had been corrected with a blue pen.

Lnguage Arts Clss Room 10.
LAnguage Arts ClAss Room 10.

A schedule was placed at each empty desk, and out of alphabetical order. It was each student's responsibility to find their assigned seat, which gave the students who were late to arrive an unfair advantage. The teacher, Mr. Garcia, a disheveled man in an amber toned cigarette-smoke smelling corduroy suit, remained seated behind his old wooden desk while the anxious grade eight students struggled to find which desk they were assigned to.

"Okay, listen here," Mr. Garcia wheezed. "I know you're all new, so I've got a few ground rules to tell you about. Follow these rules, and your next five years at K.S.S. will be easy breezy. Got it?" The students stared blankly as Mr. Garcia took a sip out of his slowly deteriorating paper coffee cup before clearing his phlegmy throat. "Rule number one. No running in the halls. That's a school rule, not one of mine. Trip for all I care. Rule number two. Don't be late for class. You've got five minutes between each class. That should be more than enough time to grab your books from your lockers and get to your next subject. I've been here for close to twenty years and haven't been late once, so if I can do it, you can do it."

Mr. Garcia's homeroom students began to fidget as they lost interest. Taylor hadn't even noticed that she had torn off the side-strips of her dot-matrix printed schedule until she began picking away at the second side.

"Rule number three. Don't smoke. But if you do, which I'm sure you will at one time or another when you want to upset mommy and daddy, or want to 'be cool'," Mr. Garcia made air-quote gestures as he spoke, "there is a smoke pit behind the school. If you can't find it, just follow your nose."

Following the third rule, the teacher proceeded to take out a newspaper. "This'll be your homeroom all year, so let's try not to get sick of each other, okay? If you leave me alone, I'll leave you alone," Mr. Garcia called out from behind the paper. Taylor wasn't sure if he was genuinely this disinterested in teaching, or if this was his weird way of trying to intimidate new students. She wondered if Mischa's homeroom teacher was any nicer.

After what felt like forever, but was only three awkward minutes of silence, Mr. Garcia proceeded to tell the class, from behind his newspaper, that "they could all leave if they wanted, he wasn't their boss." Everyone got up cautiously. *Was this a trap? Were they really allowed to leave class early?* Taylor, alongside the rest of her homeroom classmates, slowly slunk out of the classroom, and into the mostly vacant off-white hallway. The length of the halls and the expansiveness of the school's many wings were panic inducing. Taylor closed her eyes for a moment and took a deep breath. She tried to focus her thoughts. *If you get through this day, you can get through anything... Also, I wonder if the same person that painted this school painted my sister's apartment building...*

Once the anxiety faded, Taylor looked around at the other students. Everyone had mostly paired off already; friends from elementary school, she assumed. And then, she noticed *him.* The picture of perfection. Kai S-Something. Taylor had only managed to read the first part of his name when she was looking for her own schedule on the homeroom desks.

Despite Mischa's constant demands to pick out the cutest guys in Teen Beat, Taylor was never really that into boys. She knew it would happen eventually, but she still thought that they were kind of gross. But this one... He was different. Tall and lanky, with floppy black hair, in a denim jacket. Kai reminded Taylor of a skinny A.C. Slater. Determined to be the confident go-getter she knew that she had the potential to be, Taylor decided to try to talk to Kai. *He is standing alone too. Maybe he's also new to Kelowna?* she thought to herself.

"H-hey," Taylor managed to say. "Mr. Garcia is pretty weird, huh?"

"Oh, he's the worst," Kai offered. His voice was much higher pitched than Mario Lopez's but Taylor didn't mind. "I heard he once came to class drunk when his wife left him, but that could just be a rumour."

"Wow," Taylor replied.

"Did you just move here?" Kai asked, clearly disinterested but trying to be polite.

Taylor tried her best to match his chill energy level. "Oh, yeah… I moved in with my sister a month ago."

"That's what I thought. You seem pretty awkward," Kai said with a hint of judgement. "But, like, it's okay. You have all year to get better."

"Thank you?" Taylor replied with what was becoming her frequently raised eyebrow. She hoped that eyebrows couldn't build muscle mass, or half her face was going to start looking quite strange.

And with that, the tall and handsome, but surprisingly rude, Kai S-Something, walked away, leaving Taylor alone outside of Mr. Garcia's homeroom. *At least we will have homeroom together,* Taylor thought. *I'll win him over yet.* She looked down at her crumpled schedule and decided to track down her new locker, locker number 454.

◆ ◆ ◆

Mischa's morning wasn't going much better. After an awkward run in where she mistook a particularly tall twelfthgrade student for a teacher, she found herself sitting in the wrong classroom for ten minutes before realizing that it was a homeroom for special needs students. After politely excusing herself – which to Mischa meant hiding behind her hair and running out of the door as quickly as she could – she finally found the correct homeroom, at the opposite end of the building. Luckily there was only one empty desk in the otherwise cramped classroom, which meant that Mischa knew where her spot was. After quickly taking her seat, Mischa sunk down in her desk and prayed that everyone would stop looking at her. Her eyes darted around, as she tried to take in the details of the classroom. A row of grey block-like computers lined the edge of the classroom; a small green cursor bar flickered on against each monitor's black background. Mischa found herself fixated by the way that the cursors flashed ever-so-slightly out of unison. She really wished that the flashing cursors would sync up. *Huh, this must be the computer lab*, she realized, before regaining focus.

Mischa's correct homeroom teacher ended up being Ms. Bose, a very teacher-ish looking teacher with a penchant for bright primary colours and shoulder pads. She seemed normal enough, save for the open-faced egg salad sandwich that was sitting on her desk. Mischa couldn't understand who ate egg salad for breakfast, let alone open-faced. High school was a very confusing place to be.

After ten minutes of not listening to a word that Ms. Bose said, Mischa realized that she should probably try harder to pay attention. It was right then that the bell rang, and the homeroom class of thirty students poured out of the class and into the labyrinthine halls. She looked down at her class schedule and found her locker number: 455.

Following a marathon-like sprint to her locker, an enormous sense of relief washed over Mischa when she realized that her locker was next to Taylor's. The closer she got, though, the clearer she could see the look of disgust that was plastered over her friend's face.

"Hey girl, uh, what's up?" Mischa asked Taylor, who was staring deeply into the back of her wooden locker.

"I, I, I can't... Look," Taylor stammered as she turned and grabbed her friend's arm, causing Mischa to recoil ever so slightly as she really wasn't a touchy person. "I don't know what to do. I just... I just keep staring at it. Who would do this?"

"Who would do what—" Mischa's jaw dropped as she investigated the locker. What she witnessed was so much worse than being hugged in public. "Sweet Joey McIntyre," she blurted out in wide-eyed shock while staring at the horrific surprise... A sandwich bag of poop had been pinned to the back wall of the locker.

"What do I do? I can't put my stuff in there!" Taylor panicked.

"Okay, breathe…" Mischa consoled, "But not too deeply, because uh, your locker really stinks…"

"You're not helping!"

"Is that dog, or…?"

"Seriously. Stop. I'm having the worst day ever," Taylor muttered, close to tears. She had tried her best to keep it together, but this was the bag of feces that broke the camel's back… Or whatever the saying was.

"It's okay, we can just share a locker for now," Mischa offered as she slowly opened her own locker before letting out a high-pitched shriek that sounded more like a startled bird than a teenaged girl.

"Wait, what's in yours?" Taylor asked while looking into Mischa's locker, "I don't see anything…"

"Look down," Mischa spoke woefully. Taylor could feel her face turn increasingly green as she watched the pile of maggots squirming at the bottom of the locker. The mound of fly larvae writhed like a living pile of macaroni.

Suddenly, the two girls noticed that everyone in the eighth-grade locker hallway was freaking out.

"Oh my God! It smells horrible!"

"Is, is that alive?"

"I hope this is ranch dressing…"

"Why is there a naked drawing of Mr. Garcia in my locker?"

Kai S-Something stared into his locker in a way that reminded Taylor of her sister's face when she was chastised for holding hands with Tara. While he didn't scream out like the other students, Taylor knew what was in his locker must be particularly awful. "Attention all students. Please report to the gymnasium for an emergency assembly. Immediately!" An extremely unhappy voice boomed from over the intercom system.

During the standard first day of classes-turned-emergency-situation assembly, Taylor learned several key things: That the gymnasium was so large the entire school could actually fit in it, that several hundred teenagers packed into one room on a warm September day stinks worse than she ever would have assumed – perhaps even worse than her locker – and that the locker ordeal was part of an annual hazing ritual between the grade eleven students and the grade eight students. Apparently, stuff like that was normal at high school – or at least this one – and at times, even encouraged. According to the principal, who was leading the assembly, something known as the Grade Eight Play Day would be happening sometime over the next two weeks.

The details given of the Grade Eight Play Day were extremely vague, most likely to prevent the younger students from skipping classes that week. All the principal would say is that it was a "wholesome day of bonding" between the eighth and eleventh grade students, and that occasionally some kids would get taped to walls. You know, regular bonding activities. As long as no one was excessively aggressive to another student, they considered it to be "Good Clean Fun" and a rite of passage.

One particularly brave new student raised their hand.

"Yes, you?" the principal asked, who despite his large stature, looked small in the middle of the expansive gym floor.

"Why do the grade eleven students torture the eighth graders? Why not the twelfth graders? Wouldn't that make more sense as a rivalry?" the nerdy looking boy in a buttoned-up gingham print shirt asked.

"Well, that's because the senior level students have too much work on their plates, so we feel it's best to leave the fun to the grade eleven students," the principal rebutted, unphased by the use of the word 'torture'. Taylor and Mischa exchanged knowing glances with each other. Through nothing more than a nod, it was then that they decided they would definitely be skipping Grade Eight Play Day.

Chapter Seven

Exhausted and miserable after her first day of high school, Taylor was relieved that the front door to the apartment was open and that she didn't have to dig through her backpack for her key. Her feet hurt from all the walking, her clothes stunk like a combination of cheap body spray and B.O. from being around all of the other students, and she had discovered that hazing wasn't just a thing from the movies. After a day like today, even a small win like not needing to use your keys was appreciated. Taylor even found it soothing how the sound of the television emanated from the living room and into the front entrance of the apartment. The opening music of the Oprah Winfrey Show washed over her like a calming wave. Loud noises were never allowed back in the Gagnon household.

Today I am here with a very special guest. He's the twenty-six-year-old wunderkind inventor of every parent's future nightmare, the Grow a Friend toy, Doctor Phillip Austrocknung.

Future nightmare? That's not very nice of you to say, Oprah.

"Taylor! How was your first day of school? Tell me all about it!" Vanessa gushed as she ran over and gave her little sister a hug, who felt surprisingly wooden.

I say that because it's going to be a nightmare to find on store shelves!

Respectful audience laughter.

"Oh, it was alright," Taylor said apathetically as she inattentively brushed off her sister's hug, plopped her backpack on the ground, and reached into the fridge for a drink.

"Just alright?" Vanessa asked with a tone of worry that, in the moment, reminded both her and her sister of their mother, although they'd never acknowledge it.

"Don't you remember how rough school was for you, Nes?" Tara piped up, emerging from the living room.

Since the ad campaign launched this summer, shopping centres have already been fielding calls from desperate parents wondering where they'll be able to find this year's hottest toy, which you, Phillip, invented as – now stop me if I'm wrong – as a way to save your dying wife?

"It was just… it was a lot," Taylor spoke, not wanting to disappoint Vanessa. "I think I'm just going to go to my room for while, if that's okay with you?"

"Sure, no problem," Vanessa responded, trying to conceal the concern in her voice. "Do you still want to go out for dinner later? A bad first day at school is nothing that a little Chinese smorgasbord and bowling can't fix—"

"—I'm just really tired," Taylor interrupted. After all the excitement that she had been feeling earlier that day, Taylor was embarrassed that her day didn't live up to either her or her sister's expectations.

"Oh, okay. Go get some rest, and let us know if you change your mind, okay Tay?" Vanessa replied.

Tara wrapped her arm around Vanessa as Taylor went off to her room. "Jeez, poor kid must have been put through the wringer."

"I don't think I've ever seen her so bummed out before," Vanessa confessed.

"True, but you also haven't seen her much," Tara said, before immediately realizing how her words could be misinterpreted. "Look, teenagers just need space sometimes. Don't forget what you were like at that age. Every emotion is amplified by a hundred." Tara leaned in and kissed Vanessa. "Besides, we both know that going to the Chinese buffet was more for you than Taylor. If you're sad we won't be going tonight, I can go and pick-up take out."

"I love you," Vanessa replied, placing her head on Tara's shoulder as they sat back down on the couch.

"I love you, too," Tara said.

◆ ◆ ◆

Laying in the centre of her bed, Taylor stared up at the spinning ceiling fan. *Just five more years of school,* she repeated in her head, over and over with each rotation of the fan. Suddenly, Taylor found herself staring at her closet, as she remembered the purchase that she had made earlier that summer...

Accepting that she was likely influenced by the episode of Oprah her sister and Tara were playing loudly from the living room, Taylor decided to retrieve the small Grow a Friend toy that she had hidden away at the back of her closet. *It was a silly spur of the moment purchase*; she had thought at the time as she hid the package underneath her winter clothes. *No teenager needs to play with toys.* But now, feeling low, she thought it might be amusing.

Digging under the piles of pants and heavy sweaters that Taylor had carelessly left on the ground while getting ready for school, underneath the mounds of socks, sports bras, and old sneakers, she finally found what she was looking for: the slightly damaged Grow a Friend package. Taylor held the opaque egg up to the light and examined the toy. There he was: a tiny little prince dressed entirely in green. His expression was very neutral. It was difficult to tell if he was supposed to look happy or not. Taylor lowered the egg and placed it between both hands. *Here it goes,* she thought, as she cracked the egg open into two separate halves. The little prince plopped down on her bed, while his sword landed next to him.

She stared for a moment. *That's it?* Out of the corner of her eye, she noticed that a little piece of paper had also fallen out of the egg. Taylor picked it up, and squinted as she read the tiny words:

Thank you for purchasing your very own Grow a Friend ™*!*

To activate Your Friend, simply add the toy to a glass of water.

Your Friend should reach their full size within 8 to 10 hours.

Your Friend is reusable, recyclable, and non-toxic.

To store, just dehydrate. Do not microwave.

Do not iron. Made in China.

"Full size? So what, it's going to be as big as the glass? I thought that these were supposed to be friends. Like, actual full-sized friends," Taylor mumbled to herself, upset that she was swindled into buying such a cheap product, even if it was half price. *I guess it's worth a shot,* she thought as she grabbed a room temperature glass of water from her nightstand. The instructions didn't say anything about what temperature the water should be, and she was feeling kind of lazy. And so, Tay-lor dropped the tiny little prince and his sword into the glass of water. The water in the glass caused his silhouette to warp and twist as Taylor held the glass up to the light. *Alright, I guess we'll see what happens overnight.* She placed the glass back on her nightstand and decided to join Vanessa and Tara for dinner. The savoury smell of sweet and sour pork had started to creep under Taylor's bedroom door, which reminded her that she never got around to eating lunch since her appetite had been ruined by the earlier locker prank.

Chapter Eight

Uggghhhh... Taylor moaned as she rolled over to silence her alarm clock radio. The only thing worse than waking up early was the staticky lyrics to Kokomo, which were blaring next to her head. Growing up, The Beach Boys were one of the only bands that the Gagnons openly listened to, so needless to say, Taylor was not a fan. She pondered about how much a CD player alarm clock would cost as she rubbed the sleep out of her eyes. The bright red analog numbers brightly shone 7:30AM, which meant she only had half an hour to get ready before meeting Mischa downstairs.

Still groggy, Taylor reached over and turned the bedside lamp on. *Wait, where did my glass of water go?* She wondered. Had she forgotten to bring a glass to bed last night? Or maybe Vanessa came in and brought it to the kitchen? No, her sister gave her more privacy than that... Taylor slowly began to remember that she had placed the Grow a Friend in a glass of water last night. But where was it now? Just then, out of the corner of her eyes Taylor spotted something on the floor. She looked down and let out a muffled scream.

"Holy crap," she blurted out as she looked at the floor. There it was. There *he* was. The tiny prince was no longer so tiny: the Grow a Friend toy had ballooned overnight to human-size. Taylor slid off the side of the bed and onto the floor. She looked down at the life-sized and shockingly life-like prince that was laying on her bedroom floor. *I'm still dreaming, this can't be real,* Taylor tried to rationalize. She pinched her arm, leaving a bright pink mark. Okay, this wasn't a dream.

There he was, right in front of Taylor: her very own fairy-tale prince. *This is insane, oh my God,* she thought to herself. What was she going to do with a human-sized doll? How was she going to explain this to her sister and Tara? Thousands of thoughts raced through her mind and she stared into the eyes of her very own Prince Charming, only to be immediately re-placed with just one: *Wait, did he just blink?*

"Did… did you blink?" Taylor sputtered out uncertainly. *Great, now I'm talking to a toy. Maybe I've gone insane.* She looked at her alarm clock. It was 7:45AM. There were now only fif-teen minutes to get ready for school, and Taylor either had a life-sized royal on her floor or was hallucinating. It was only two days into the school year, and she had already cracked. *Just great…* Taylor reached over and touched the Grow a Friend's arm. It was much squishier than expected; some water squeezed out as she gripped around his forearm. Despite his life-like appearance, the Grow a Friend toy was most certainly made of sponge.

"He's just a sponge... He isn't alive. You're just over-tired and imagining things," Taylor said while standing up and walking towards her mirror. She looked closely at her reflection and pinched her cheek. *Okay, that one hurt too.* At least she wasn't still dreaming. Hopefully Tara and Vanessa made extra coffee this morning, she was going to need it... Just then, there was a loud knock at her bedroom door.

"Yo Taylor, were you just going to leave me waiting in the lobby?" Mischa's knock on the faux-wood bedroom door caused the Grow a Friend to immediately sit up, nearly giving Taylor a heart attack as she caught his reflection from behind her in the mirror.

Beep, beep, beep... Mischa rolled over and hit the off button on her alarm clock as it brightly flashed 6:30AM. The alarm used to bug her when she was younger, but she had grown used to it over the years and now routinely woke up a good ten or fifteen minutes early. Her dad used to wake up even earlier to make Mischa and her brother Michael breakfast, but since he switched careers and started working nights at the hospital, the Jones siblings needed to get ready on their own. At least they lived in downtown Kelowna now, which made things easier for everyone. As cramped as their three-bedroom apartment was, Mischa liked living downtown. It made her feel like she was a part of something, instead of just existing on the outskirts of town, back when they lived in a small house across the Okanagan Lake Bridge in Westbank.

Mischa got out of bed and stretched. Her small black-polished fingernails nearly touched the ceiling if she stretched hard enough. Maybe one day she'd be able to touch the popcorn sprayed ceiling, but today wasn't the day. She changed her flannel pajamas for a pair of black pants and a black sweater and walked over to her brother Michael's room. "Get up or you're going to miss your bus!" Mischa yelled. Michael had transferred from K.S.S. and now went to another high school in town, and it was somehow Mischa's responsibility to make sure that he was awake in time. He did not inherit the early-riser genes that the other Jones' had.

Jones wasn't their family's original name. The original name was something in Nsyilxcen, but it was lost when Mischa's grandpa was sent to a residential school. That's about all Mischa knew about her family's history; that, and her mom passed away when she was little. Her dad was very much a forward thinker, which unfortunately meant that he didn't like to talk much about the past. Mischa found his mentality frustrating, even if she was sometimes the same way. She desperately wanted to know more about her mom and her history but conceded that she would probably never find out. Since her dad started working as a nurse, she felt like she barely saw him anymore.

Mischa reached into the cupboard and pulled out a bright box of Froot Loops. She and Michael used to argue about which colours tasted the best, before their dad made them do a blind taste test thus proving that they were all the same flavour. While annoyed with her dad at first, Mischa eventually forgave him. She liked *froot* flavour, whatever it was supposed to be.

Michael stumbled out of his bedroom. Mischa thought that his gross teenaged mustache made him look like he had dirt on face. "I told you to wash your face," Mischa mocked as Michael sat across from her at the kitchen table and poured himself a bowl of cereal.

"I can shave this off, but no matter what, you'll still be ugly," Michael retorted with a smile before letting out a loud burp. "I thought Dad told you to start wearing more colour? You look like something that crawled out of an Anne Rice novel."

"If you rat on me, I'll tell him what you keep under your mattress," Mischa replied between bites of cereal.

"Wait, how do you know I have those?" Michael replied, flustered.

Mischa smirked from behind her long hair as she brought her empty bowl to the kitchen sink. She looked at the time on the stove. 7:30AM. Taylor was only five minutes away, but Mischa figured she might as well leave early.

"I'm just kidding, you aren't late. I'm early," Mischa called out from behind Taylor's bedroom door. "You going to let me in though, or what?" Taylor sat face to face with her life-sized Grow a Friend prince while Mischa continued to beckon.

"Uhhh, just a minute... I need to, uh, get dressed," Taylor yelled back. She should have known that this would happen. The advertising said repeatedly that Grow a Friends would allow you to, well, grow a friend. Advertisements always lie though – how was she supposed to know that this would be the one time a toy was actually *under* hyped?

"Oh come on, it's nothing I haven't seen before," Mischa said as she began to open the door. Not knowing what to do, Taylor grabbed the neon orange comforter from her bed and threw it over the Grow a Friend.

"Who the hell is hiding under your blanket?" Mischa asked bluntly while sitting on the side of Taylor's bed. The orange blanket did nothing to conceal the Grow a Friend. On the contrary, it drew attention to him. Feeling silly, Taylor scrambled to think of how to explain her bizarre morning...

"There is so much I need to tell you! So, in the summer, I wandered into San Francisco Gifts and—"

"—And you met a boy, whatever. Who is it? I hope he's cute—" Mischa interrupted Taylor as she pulled off the blanket that was concealing the Grow a Friend. "Eww, why's your blanket wet?" she blurted out, more perturbed by the blanket's moisture level than by the random prince that was directly in front of her.

"That's part of what I needed to explain," Taylor sighed. She knew Mischa was someone she could trust, but this was such a bizarre situation that Taylor wasn't sure what to think anymore.

"Okay, I'm all ears," Mischa replied, while the reality that she was staring at someone dressed as a prince began to sink in.

"So... I went to the mall and... Just look. Um. He's a Grow a Friend," Taylor conceded.

"A Grow a Friend... Okay, that makes sense, I guess... But I thought they weren't going to be released for another two months?" Mischa asked skeptically.

"How are you more shocked that I bought a toy before anyone else than there being a life-sized prince on my floor?" Taylor retorted. This was not the response that she had expected from Mischa.

The Grow a Friend remained completely still as the two friends stared at him. His red hair and ginger complexion contrasted boldly against his green prince outfit. Despite the impressive nature of his existence, he looked as if he was designed by someone that had read every single fairy-tale and was told to make the most generic looking royal possible, but with dimples.

"He's so real looking..." Mischa cooed while reaching out to touch the Grow a Friend's extremely smooth and spongey face.

"That's the thing, Meesh. I think he *is* real."

"Yeah, real wet," Mischa retorted, slightly disgusted while flinging water off her fingertips. Despite his human appearance, the Grow a Friend was coated in a clear film.

"No. Real, real," Taylor replied adamantly. The tone in her voice reminded her of the crazed people who walked around with signs proclaiming that the world was ending. She hoped that Mischa wasn't thinking the same thing.

"I mean, isn't that the point of these toys?" Mischa pressed. "You know, to be life-like?"

"Yeah, life-LIKE!" Taylor protested. "Not actually living. I saw him blink!"

"Are you sure you're not imagining things? Also, why is he dressed like Robin Hood?" Mischa said while sliding down from the side of the bed and on to the floor. She stared into the Grow a Friend's eyes. "I don't see any blinks, just way too much green for one man's wardrobe." Mischa reached over and poked the Grow a Friend's spongey nose, before turning back to Taylor. "That's the thing about Grow a Friends. They're supposed to be realistic! Man, you're so lucky. Everyone is going to be so jealous of you—" Mischa instantly fell silent as the Grow a Friend reached forward and poked her nose. His damp finger left a small drop of water behind, which rolled off of the end of Mischa's nose.

"Your... Your Grow a Friend touched me... D-did you see that?" Mischa stammered, while hopping up and running towards Taylor's bedroom door. Taylor was extremely relieved that she wasn't actually insane.

Taylor leaned towards the totally real and non-hallucinatory Grow a Friend, who hadn't moved since poking Mischa. "Are you alive?" she asked. The Grow a Friend slowly lifted his arm and pointed at himself. "Yes, you," Taylor pressed.

"I… alive." The Grow a Friend slowly spoke in an oddly high-pitched British accent. He really was a very cliché prince.

The Grow a Friend then slowly pointed at Taylor who responded uncertainly, "Yes, I am alive too. My name is Taylor. That's my friend Mischa over there."

"Meeesha," the Grow a Friend replied, "Tay-lor…" The prince spoke as if he was a family friendly version of Frankenstein's monster.

"That's right," Taylor spoke encouragingly. "What is your name?"

"My… name?" the Grow a Friend replied, confused.

"Yes, your name," Mischa replied, having rejoined Taylor next to the Grow a Friend.

The Grow a Friend didn't respond. After several moments, flickers of cognition began happening from behind the Grow a Friend's previously vacant stare. "My, name… Yes… I have a name… I remember now…" The Grow a Friend spoke softly as he began to recall his name. He paused for a moment, choosing his next words carefully. "I am Prince Alexander Charming, Son of… Another Charming…" The Grow a Friend froze as he struggled to remember a past that he never lived.

"I don't think he's a real prince," Mischa whispered to Taylor. While her tone was sarcastic, her words were not.

"Silence, wench!" Alexander demanded-slash-squeaked, springing to his feet and catching both of the girls off-guard. "You shall not disrespect a royal in such a way! Now, where is my sword…" The spongey prince frantically looked around for his sword, before picking it up off of the floor and lunging towards Mischa. It would have been much more intimidating if the sword wasn't made of sponge and didn't have an empty glass stuck to the end of it.

"Prince... Alexander, was it?" Taylor spoke calmly, while leaning forward and pulling the glass off of the Prince's hydrated sword. "Mischa didn't mean to be rude."

"I just say dumb things! I'm sorry!" Mischa said from behind Taylor's comforter, which she was now holding up as a shield. She lowered the blanket when she realized that the sword was made of sponge and was likely as dangerous as a child's bath toy.

Alexander looked back and forth between the two girls. He lowered the sword as he realized that they were clearly no threat. "Alright. I accept your apologies, wench."

"Could you please stop calling us wenches?" Taylor asked.

"I would never call you a wench, m'lady," Alexander said while taking Taylor's hand. "Just her," he said, gesturing towards Mischa with his chiseled chin.

Ignoring Alexander's insult, Mischa leaned towards Taylor. "This might be an awkward time to bring this up, but we're going to be seriously late for school." Mischa was many things: awkward goth kid, friend, sister, daughter, face to face with a recently animated sponge-being... But she wasn't someone who was okay with being late to school. Yesterday's homeroom experience was bad enough.

"Oh no! You're right," Taylor realized. "I know we just met, Alexander, but my um... wench, and I need to leave to go to, ummm... another castle," she consoled the confused prince the best that she could, which was a challenge seeing as she could use some consoling herself.

"I understand. A brave warrior princess like you, miss Taylor, must have many duties to see to," Alexander said while letting go of Taylor's hand.

"I'll be back later this afternoon. Please stay here and, uh—" Taylor said while flicking a drop of water from her fingertips. She wondered if her hand felt as alien to Alexander Charming as his hand felt to her. She paused for a moment as she struggled to come up with something to placate the recently animated sponge prince, "—guard this room, I guess?"

"You have my word," Alexander vowed.

"One more thing..." Mischa mumbled as she passed Alexander a bath towel that was hung on the back of Taylor's bedroom door, "You should use this."

"Thank you, Mischa," Alexander spoke. Mischa knew that she shouldn't care so much about the opinions of a boy that had only recently come to life, but she was happy that he didn't call her a wench that time.

Prince Alexander grew concerned as Taylor and Mischa began to leave the bedroom. "Do you know how I got here?" he asked sincerely, while taking in his surroundings.

"We'll talk more when I get home," Taylor said, while slowly closing the door. At least she and Mischa had gotten the weirdest part of their days over with before nine in the morning; they were both confident it would be smooth sailing from there.

Chapter Nine

The morning seemed to drag on and on... Fortunately, the first class of the day was only an introductory gym class. It was also one of the two classes that Taylor and Mischa had together; Science was the other. Seeing as it was only two days into the school year, the coach used this class time to point out the basic things like where the change rooms were located, what the pieces of equipment were called, and how important it was to never, under any circumstance, run in the school halls. The constant reiteration about the importance of not running in the school halls made Taylor wonder if something had happened in the past that caused this rule. Her father always said that there was a story behind every rule, which made her think that this rule must have a doozy of a story... Following the brief introduction to the school's gymnasium equipment, all of the students were led over to a giant cork bulletin board where they were prompted to sign up for the school's sports teams.

"Yay, mandatory fun," Mischa quipped while not so subtly rolling her eyes.

"What are you signing up for?" Taylor asked with a tone of uncertainty.

"I hate team sports," Mischa mumbled as she stood awkwardly in her nylon gym shorts and oversized t-shirt.

"So… Track?" Taylor rebutted.

"Is that one of the options?" Mischa asked while scanning the sign-up sheets that were affixed with mismatched plastic tacks.

"Hey Stretch, I sure hope you're signing up for basketball!" The coach mused as he walked by Taylor. His potbelly combined with his all-too-white running shoes made Taylor think that he hadn't participated in many sports himself recently. Despite his shape, the coach had walked away before Taylor could think of a reply.

"Stretch? How original," Mischa said to Taylor, defensively.

"I've gotten used to stuff like that…" Taylor confided. "I'm definitely not signing up for basketball now though."

"What about cross country running?" Mischa offered. "We could both sign up and just like, walk?"

Taylor shrugged in agreement while reaching for the blue gel pen that was tied to the bulletin board with a piece of butcher's string and scrawled her name at the top of the running team list: *Taylor Gagnon.*

"Gagnon? More like *gagged*-on!" Lauren Daniels, a waspy girl with unnaturally yellow hair mocked. It was obvious that Lauren had experimented with Kool Aid as hair dye in the summer, and it hadn't fully washed out. *Is this my first bully?* Taylor mused.

"No, just Gagnon… It's French," Taylor replied casually. If there was one thing that she had learned from after school specials, it was to never react emotionally to a bully; reacting would only make the bullying worse. While typically the first to respond to a bully, this time Mischa was frozen in her place, like a deer hoping not to be seen by a hunter.

"Oh, well *au revoir* then, Taylor Gagged-on. And Mischa, nice to see you're still an ugly little dweeb," Lauren snarked as she walked away and rejoined her gaggle of friends, which happened to be entirely boys. The way that her extremely thin legs protruded from her oversized gym shorts reminded Taylor of a toddler that was playing dress up in their parents' clothing. The way that the boys in gym class interacted with her though, showed that they didn't harbour the same opinions of her new bully. Taylor watched as Lauren talked to the group of boys, which included Kai S-Something; the way that Kai and the other boys held on to Lauren's every word and laughed, seemingly on cue, made Taylor deeply insecure.

Taylor turned to Mischa, who was finally defrosting from her interaction with Lauren the ice queen. "What was that about?"

"I was afraid that this would happen… I understand if you don't want to be my friend anymore…" Mischa mumbled while walking towards the gymnasium change rooms. Tears began to well up, which she tried the best she could to hide behind her bangs.

"What? Don't be ridiculous!" Taylor called out while in pursuit. "Why wouldn't I want to be your friend?"

"Because I'm a target and hanging out with me will make you a target, too," Mischa admitted while opening her gym locker and changing as quickly as she could.

"Meesh, the bell hasn't even gone yet, you're going to get in trouble—" Taylor said, while also putting her gym clothes away. If Mischa was going to get detention, so would she.

"Lauren is the worst of the worst, you don't want her in your life," Mischa spoke while holding in tears.

"No, but I want you in my life," Taylor said calmingly. "You're my friend! I'm not going to ditch you because some random person said something mean to me."

"Thank you, Taylor," Mischa sniffled. "You're my friend too." The two friends sat down on the wooden change room benches.

"What happened between you two?" Taylor asked.

"Where to start... Well, three years ago, back in fifth grade, I told her that a song she chose to play at the school dance sucked. Rude, I guess, but whatever. After that, she has done everything she can to make my life hell. It's literally her hobby. In grade six, she put glue in my hair... Uh, she pants-ed me during volleyball... And then last year, she got caught with some weird diet pills, and told everyone my brother had sold them to her. She had never even met my brother before."

"Jesus," Taylor exclaimed.

"Yeah... He had to switch schools over her. Hate is a strong word but, Taylor, I *hate* her," Mischa confided, no longer crying. "She's a little rich kid so I figured her parents would send her to a private school this year, but I guess not."

"I'm here though," Taylor offered. "You have a friend now. You're not alone. I've got your back." She wasn't sure if those were the right words to say, but she meant it.

"Thanks dude," Mischa said, regaining confidence. "Let's get out of here before gym class ends and we run into her again, though." Just as the two girls left the change room, the second period bell rang. *Home free*, Taylor thought, as she shielded Mischa from Lauren's view and they exited the gym.

Just as Taylor and Mischa were sitting down in the cafeteria, Vanessa and Tara were walking home together for lunch. It didn't happen often, but that afternoon was one of the rare times when their work schedules lined up completely.

"You know, I could have made you lunch at the café," Tara offered, trying to conceal that she was getting winded as she walked quickly alongside her much faster partner. The entire Gagnon family was lanky and had the minor superpower of walking slightly faster than most people.

"I know you would have, but then we wouldn't be taking lunch together, would we?" Vanessa offered, her long legs easily striding across the sidewalk, careful to avoid stepping on any of the cracks. She couldn't help herself. It was a weird little tic she had had since childhood.

]"But then you'd get a longer break and we wouldn't have to walk so fast to get home," Tara wheezed. Vanessa slowed down. She often forgot how much taller she was than Tara, and really didn't mean to walk so quickly. "That's better," Tara conceded.

Suddenly, Vanessa came to a complete stop, only half a block away from their apartment. "Oh, come on, I'm not that out of shape, I don't need to stop for a rest," Tara teased. Her tone shifted when she realized that Vanessa wasn't smiling. "Uh, babe… What's wrong?"

"Do you see that?" Vanessa said with a hushed breath.

"See what?"

"Look up at Taylor's window," Vanessa said, pointing into the distance. "There's someone in there."

Vanessa and Tara both began sprinting to the Manhattan Manor at full speed. After fumbling with the front door keys, Tara hurried into the elevator, while Vanessa booked it up the stairs like Rocky Balboa. Feeling a tinge of guilt from choosing to take the elevator, Tara rapidly pushed the old sticky third-floor button in a failed attempt to move faster. Somehow, they both reached the third floor at the same time.

"Wait!" Tara whisper-yelled. "We can't just barge in; we need a plan!" she said while instinctively placing her keyring between her fingers like a Wolverine claw.

Vanessa paused. "You're right…" she whispered as she dug through her purse.

"What are you doing?" Tara asked.

"Grabbing this," Vanessa proclaimed while showing Tara the small cartridge of pepper spray she kept in the bottom of her bag.

"Where did you get that?" Tara asked.

"That's not important right now," Vanessa said defensively, while proceeding to put her key in the lock. She didn't want to explain to Tara that she had been secretly packing pepper spray since she first moved to the city at sixteen.

Vanessa opened the door slowly, while holding the pepper spray in front of her. She really hoped that it would work as a deterrent, because spraying it indoors would cause it to get in her and Tara's eyes as well. Once on the other side of the apartment door, she could see a shadow from someone's feet pacing in front of Taylor's bedroom door. "Hey loser! I see you! Get the hell out of there!" Vanessa called out with a ferocity that made Tara think she probably didn't need that pepper spray. The shadow stopped pacing.

"I have been instructed to guard this room!" an unexpectedly high-pitched male British voice yelled back.

Tara and Vanessa looked at each other, confused. "'Instructed to guard this room?' That's a new one. The phone is in the kitchen, I'm going to call the police," Vanessa called out, while reaching for the phone that was affixed to the wall by the fridge. She passed the pepper spray to Tara, who proceeded to point it at the bedroom door. Tara hated weapons, but internally accepted that the pepper spray would be much more effective than the small apartment keys that she was still holding between her fingers.

"Perhaps I should be the one calling the police, seeing as you are the intruders!" the cracking British voice called back, with a slight tinge of uncertainty. Tara and Vanessa exchanged confused glances.

"I knew we should have moved last year when our lease renewed," Tara mumbled.

"Listen, let's make a deal. We won't call the cops if you just leave. We don't want any trouble," Vanessa called out to the mysterious intruder.

"You listen!" the voice called back, having shaken their previously uncertain tone. "I was asked to guard this room on order of Princess Taylor, and I will not fail her."

"Princess… Taylor?" Vanessa questioned, while hanging the phone back up on its receiver. A wave of relief washed over her. "Tara, it has got to be one of Taylor's new friends."

"New friend? She's only had one day of school."

"New friend, random weirdo, whatever. It's clearly some kid from her school. Probably an awkward exchange student," Vanessa whispered, while sneaking towards Taylor's bedroom door. "You mentioned Princess Taylor," Vanessa called out. "She's my little sister."

The mysterious figure waited several moments before answering, "How do I know you're telling the truth?"

"You'll just have to trust me, I guess," Vanessa asserted. "I'm opening up the door now…"

Vanessa and Tara slowly opened Taylor's bedroom door, revealing a stoic but slightly tired looking Prince Alexander Charming. They stared at the prince, confused, while Alexander looked the two of them up and down.

"Hmm, yes. I see it. You are clearly an older version of Princess Taylor," Alexander said with a nod. "And this must be your trusted farm hand."

"You should talk, you're dressed like Peter Pan," Tara retorted.

"Peter Pan? No, no. My name is Prince Alexander Charming and I—"

"—Look, I don't know what's going on, how you got in here, or why you're dressed like that, but you need to leave," Vanessa interrupted. She only had half an hour for lunch before she needed to go back to work, and was less than impressed that she was having to waste most of her break talking to some obviously unstable kid.

"I can't leave without Taylor's permission," Alexander argued.

"Yes, you can, and will. You're what, sixteen? Seventeen? You are *way* too old to be hanging out with my little sister."

"I am..." Alexander paused. "I... I don't know how old I am."

Tara turned to Vanessa and whispered in her ear, "He's clearly not alright, I don't feel good about kicking this kid onto the street." Vanessa proceeded to sit on Taylor's bed, and gestured to Alexander that he should do the same. Alexander grabbed the towel from the floor and placed it under himself before sitting on the bed. Tara watched all of this from the doorway, feeling a confusing combination of bemusement and worry.

"Why don't you tell me who you are, and how you know Taylor?" Vanessa asked calmly.

"As I was saying, my name is Prince Alexander Charming. I met Taylor this morning when she discovered me on her bedroom floor—"

"Okay perv, you need to get out of here—" Tara spouted while preparing to grab Alexander's collar. Thankfully Vanessa stopped her before she could reach his neck; Tara was a good foot shorter than this man, there was no way she could physically remove him like she had wanted to.

"I didn't mean to upset you! My memory is very foggy. I am remembering little bits here and there, but that's all. I swear to you, m'ladies, that I am telling you the truth as I see it," Alexander pleaded. "I woke up on the floor, that is all I remember. That, and I…" His voice trailed off as he scanned the room. "I came from this egg!" The young prince proclaimed while holding up his plastic Grow a Friend package.

"You came from a plastic egg?" Tara retorted, while taking the egg from the prince's hands and examining it. She wasn't sure what kind of drugs this kid was on, but clearly he was unwell.

"Yes, I recognise how bizarre it is that a royal like myself would travel in such a thrifty container, but I swear to you, I came from that egg," Alexander continued to plead. Just then, Vanessa noticed something along the back of his neck. A tattoo?

"Hold still," Vanessa said, while reaching towards the prince's neck. "What's this?" She also wanted to know why his skin was so damp but thought it would be weird to ask.

"What's what?" Alexander asked. Vanessa stood him up and walked him towards Taylor's full-length mirror. She then reached into her purse and proceeded to pull out a small make-up mirror, so that Alexander could see the back of his neck. Yes, there it was in plain black text: YOUR FRIEND ™ 1994.

"Nes..." Tara spoke warily. She held the plastic egg alongside the reflection of Alexander's neck. While written in much smaller letters, it shared the same trademark stamp. Maybe the guy in front of them wasn't lying...

"If you're no longer going to kick me out, then could you please be so kind as to bring me a glass of water? I am very thirsty," Alexander asked, while Vanessa and Tara stared at each other in shock. To make matters even stranger, they could both swear that Alexander had aged several years over the course of their conversation. His once smooth face was looking increasingly sunken.

"Sure, I'll uh, be right back," Vanessa sputtered, as she rushed to the kitchen to get Alexander a large glass of water. Alexander graciously accepted the glass, before sticking his right hand into it, and absorbing the contents. And with that, Alexander once again looked like a thirteen-year-old boy.

"Thank you," Alexander spoke sincerely, his young voice cracking. "I really needed that."

Chapter Ten

Mr. Hanes' piece of chalk scratched across the board rapidly as if the teacher's hand was possessed. His navy-blue sweater sleeves dragged across the board, occasionally erasing parts of the words he had previously completed. Taylor was baffled that someone could know so much about one subject, especially something as complicated as eighth grade science. At the start of class, Mr. Hanes had enthusiastically announced that the class was to learn all about human anatomy. Not just the basics like what the heart is, but how all of the organs are connected to larger systems. The only thing that Taylor knew about the circulatory system was that her heart pounded when she was anxious and that old people should eat less salt. And now she was supposed to learn how it was all connected? After the earlier excitement of having her Grow a Friend come to life, and now the disappointing reality of having a school bully, Taylor struggled to care about schoolwork. She was never going to be able to explain things to her sister…

Mischa, on the other hand, was fascinated by everything that the teacher was saying. Science was one of the few topics that actually held her interest. She was eager to learn how the human body worked, and how it was all connected. Because she never really felt like she fit in, there was something reassuring to Mischa to know that underneath, everyone was just a skeleton. She tried her best to take notes and write down everything that felt like it would be on a future test. Her purple gel pen smoothly scrawled across the pages of paper in her binder as Mr. Hanes continued to speak at a rapid pace. All of a sudden, Mischa's focus was broken by a hushed whisper.

"I'm sorry, could you pass me my pencil? It's by your feet."

Without turning back to acknowledge the whisperer, Mischa looked down at her black and white Converse sneakers and spotted a chewed-on pencil. She picked it up, assuming that any saliva on the pencil had rubbed off on to the classroom's old brown carpet, and turned around to return it to its owner.

"Thank you," the nerdy boy said, as his brown eyes locked with Mischa's through her black bangs. Mischa wasn't great with faces, but could remember this boy from yesterday's emergency assembly. It helped that he was once again in a buttoned-up gingham print shirt.

"No problem," she retorted, before nervously looking away and turning her focus back to Mr. Hanes' lecture. She felt a small smile wash over her face.

"I'm Benjamin," he whisper-called out to Mischa.

As if someone had pressed pause on a VCR, Mr. Hanes abruptly stopped his lesson. "Excuse me, you two. Is there something you'd like to share with the class?" he asked, perturbed.

To Mischa's relief, Benjamin piped up first. "It's my fault, I just dropped my pencil."

"Sounded like more than that. Next time, pick it up, and move on. You can chat on your own time," the teacher retorted with his hands on his hips. His chalky fingertips left an accidental smudge on his black slacks.

Mischa wasn't sure if her heart was pounding because she almost got detention, or because she had her very first crush that wasn't just on a celebrity from Tiger Beat. She couldn't wait to tell Taylor all about it on their walk home. Just as she picked up her pen to continue taking notes, the bell rang.

"That's all for today," Mr. Hanes called out, knowing that no one was really listening to him. The classroom full of bored and tired teenagers scrambled out as quickly as they could. Mischa and Taylor blended in with the crowd of their peers. "I swear everyday won't be so note heavy and you'll see that science can be fun!" His voice broke slightly as he said 'fun'. After a decade of teaching eighth graders, he knew that he should lower his expectations, but it still bothered him how little most of them cared. After the last student had cleared out, Mr. Hanes sat down at his desk and began to work on the next day's lesson. He was thankful it was a short week.

"Taylor, slow down!" Mischa called out as Taylor rushed to her locker.

"I've got to get home before my sister does!" Taylor yelled to Mischa, without looking back.

"Why?" Mischa asked, before immediately realizing that was a stupid question.

"Seriously?" Taylor asked, dumbfounded.

"Sorry, sorry… I got distracted," Mischa apologized.

Taylor looked at her friend with a hint of concern. Was Mischa's attention span really that terrible? "It's okay, today was a long day. We've got to get home to Alexander though. My sister and Tara will lose their minds if they find out I have a stranger in my room!" This outburst caused several eavesdropping students to do double takes, which neither Taylor nor Mischa noticed. The two girls grabbed their backpacks, slammed their lockers closed in unison, and made a bee-line through the crowds and out K.S.S.'s massive front doors.

That afternoon, the entrance to the Manhattan Manor felt particularly imposing. The enchantment of the name had worn off, and in this moment, the building's five storeys' worth of brown walls loomed over Taylor in a way that made her feel like she was walking into a giant cardboard box.

"Are you sure you don't want me to come with you? What if your sister doesn't believe you?" Mischa offered while picking at her increasingly chipped black nail polish.

"If my sister doesn't believe that my Grow a Friend came to life and I'm not actually holding some random British guy hostage in my room, I don't know how you will help to convince her," Taylor replied with a sigh.

"I mean, I wouldn't mind watching you try to explain it to her," Mischa retorted, "Plus I'm your friend so like, I should probably be there for you. We could also hide him at my place?"

Even though she knew Mischa's intentions were pure, Taylor was happy to have her friend by her side as they climbed the stairs up to unit 315. Vanessa and Tara usually didn't get home until about four or five, and it was three-thirty now, according to Taylor's watch. All she had to do was get home before her sister, convince the Grow a Friend not to attack them with his spongey sword, and think of a convincing argument on why she should be allowed to keep him, all in thirty minutes... Easy-peasy.

As Taylor reached the apartment, she noticed light faintly shining under the door. Someone was in the kitchen. "Oh, shi—" Taylor started to mutter, right as the apartment door swung open and she came face to face with Vanessa, Tara, and Prince Alexander.

"Hey, the gang's all here," Mischa blurted out. "I should go home... My dad will be mad... Uh, see you tomorrow, Tay," she mumbled as she turned and hurried back towards the stairs.

"Hey little sis, we need to have a talk," Vanessa said. Her voice was much softer than Taylor anticipated. At best, she had messed up and wasted her money on a stupid toy, at worst Vanessa probably thought she was hiding a boy in her room; why wasn't her sister yelling at her?

"I'm sorry, I'll go to my room," Taylor said, trying to conceal the knot of sadness that was building in her throat.

"What? Kiddo, you're not in trouble," Tara piped up.

"Mom and Dad really did a number on you," Vanessa offered sympathetically, while putting her arm around Taylor and leading her inside.

"If you're not mad at me, why did you bombard me at the door?" Taylor asked as she tightly clutched a bottle of Clearly Canadian that Tara had brought her from the fridge. Her long boney fingers grew increasingly cold as the condensation formed around the bottle. She looked over at Alexander, who was also holding a bottle of the soda. Had his hands grown larger, or was she imagining things?

"Honestly, we were just trying to be funny," Vanessa said. The rag tag group of women and a spongey prince were now all seated in the living room. "At first, we were pretty shocked when we discovered Prince Alex here, but once we realized that he's a Grow a Friend and not a creepy exchange student that you brought home, we calmed down."

Taylor couldn't believe what she was hearing. She was so used to being yelled at when she lived with her parents, it hadn't even crossed her mind that her sister wouldn't be upset with her.

"I want you to know, Princess Taylor, that I did the best I could to defend your room," Alexander offered.

"He really did," Tara added.

"Swish, swish!" Alexander said as he jokingly swung around his spongey sword which had now shrunken back down to its original pre-hydrated size. Everyone laughed, except for Taylor who was still dumbfounded.

"This just really isn't how I expected things to play out," Taylor spoke. She couldn't think of another time that she had been as relieved as she was in that moment.

Chapter Eleven

After what was perhaps the most bizarre day of her life, Taylor was extremely happy to crawl into bed. Not only had her discounted Grow a Friend toy come to life after all, but she finally understood that she was living somewhere safe. She could confide in her big sister, and close her eyes safely at night without worrying about being scolded because she had forgotten to put away her dinner dishes or some other trivial problem. After spending the entire day dreading a confrontation with her sister, she was immensely relieved that they had all spent the evening talking with Alexander and teaching him about the world that he was just brought into. It was odd at first, trying to teach a recently animated spongey-being about society – it took some time to convince him that he wasn't actually a prince and no, dragons were not an imminent threat – but by the end of the night, Taylor, Vanessa, Tara, and Alexander, were acting like family. While there would be quirks to work out along the way, they had decided that Alexander could stay with them for as long as he wanted. Tara and Vanessa had debated reporting this incident to the Grow a Friend company, but didn't want to have to return Alexander to the store or something. The people at San Francisco Gifts would probably dehydrate him and send him back to the manufacturers... The very idea of that sent shivers down their spines. Besides, the advertisements did say that the toys were meant to 'be lifelike.' What was more 'lifelike' that a living person? Nope, the Grow a Friend company would never find out.

That night, Taylor's pink sheets and orange comforter felt especially soft and cozy. She pulled the covers over her head, and closed her eyes. Tomorrow was Friday, which meant she just had to get through one more day of classes before it would be her very first weekend as a high school student. Taylor assumed that she wasn't going to be invited to any crazy parties like in the movies, but she also hadn't expected to now be friends with a real-life Prince Charming. *The world is full of surprises,* Taylor thought as she dozed off.

Alexander didn't need sleep, at least, not that he knew of. Perhaps sleep was something that would come later, but for now, it was decided that he would stay up at night watching TV and taking in as much as he could about the world he now lived in. Vanessa and Tara blocked out a few of the channels though, to keep him safe.

Taylor's alarm went off at 7:30AM as it did every morning. She stretched and rubbed her eyes, as she gradually began to remember the previous day's events. *It all happened, right?* She looked over at Alexander's plastic egg that was still sitting on her night stand. *Yep, yesterday was definitely real.*

Taylor stumbled out of her bedroom and into the kitchen where she poured herself a cup of the coffee that Tara had left brewing. Tara and Vanessa couldn't decide if thirteen-year-olds should have caffeine or not, but figured it wasn't the worst thing that Taylor could drink. Considering she was only a few inches shy of being six feet tall, it's not like it would be that bad if her growth was stunted. Taylor reached into the fridge and grabbed the carton of milk, which she poured directly into her cup of coffee. Even though she had slept extremely well that night, Taylor really felt like she needed a cup of coffee before she went into the living room to check on Alexander. To be honest, she wasn't really sure if she liked coffee, or just felt like she was supposed to. Like with green apple flavoured candy. Just as the first taste of the slightly acidic coffee hit her lips, Taylor was suddenly greeted with an enthusiastic "Good morning!" from right behind her.

"Oh my God!" Taylor jumped, spilling coffee on her pink plaid pajamas.

"Oh my God!" Prince Alexander mimicked. "You are so funny! You are a regular Elaine."

"Did you stay up all night watching Seinfeld?" Taylor asked.

"Seinfeld, something about a loud lady as well... Rosies? I also stumbled across a fascinating program... called... What is it where they ask for a credit card number?" Alexander excitedly explained in his over-the-top British accent as he and Taylor made their way to the kitchen table.

"An infomercial?" Taylor replied with a hint of concern as she took another sip of coffee.

"Yes! I found an infomercial starring the old gentleman from a Star Trek show, which I also watched. The infomercial was proclaiming that, through the power of mail, I could attend school! Taylor, I have decided, I want to go to school too," Alexander spoke sincerely.

Taylor wanted to say yes, he should definitely attend school, but Alexander wasn't a real kid... Was he? He certainly seemed real. But according to the government and the school board, Taylor wasn't sure if he would "count," as awful as that was for her to consider. "Let's talk to Vanessa and Tara when they get home," she instead replied. Sure, she was a teenager now, but this felt like something that needed an adult answer. Alexander nodded.

"Have you eaten breakfast?" Taylor asked.

"No, not yet. I don't think I need to eat, actually. Although I'd be happy to try some orange juice. It is an essential part of a balanced breakfast!"

Taylor poured Alexander a glass of orange juice, which he proceeded to stick his hand into and absorb. "Delicious," he proclaimed, as he walked over to the sink to wash off the remaining pulp that was stuck to his fingers. Taylor stared, wide-eyed, as she finished off the last few sips of her coffee.

The clock on the microwave caught Taylor's attention – she had fixed it shortly after moving in so it no longer aggressively flashed 12:00 – it was time to meet Mischa for their walk to school. "I've got to go to school. Are you sure you're going to be okay home alone?" Taylor asked with a hint of concern.

"Absolutely, m'lady. As long as I have things to watch, I will be okay," Alexander replied earnestly.

Taylor felt terrible about leaving him alone all day, but Vanessa, Tara, and her all had lives that they needed to live. If Alexander was certain that he would be okay at home, they were going to have to trust him. She gestured towards the microwave, "I will be home when that says three-thirty."

Alexander stared at her blankly. Taylor realized that she had confused him, so she reached into the kitchen's junk drawer and pulled out a pad of paper and a pen which she used to write 3:30 in giant numbers. "I will be home when the clock has these numbers on it."

As soon as Taylor left the apartment, a weird sensation washed over Alexander. Something melancholic… "Is this what being sad feels like?" Alexander reflected out loud. "But what reason do I have to be unhappy?"

It wasn't sadness that he was experiencing, but seeing as he had only been brought into this world 36 hours prior, he was still struggling to understand his feelings. Why did Taylor leaving Alexander home alone make him feel this particular way? It was as if something was missing in his insides. On television, everyone was always happy, sad, or in the case of the late-night court shows Alexander had discovered: angry. He wasn't feeling any of those three things though.

Having enjoyed his earlier drink, Alexander poured himself another glass of orange juice, and took a seat back in front of the TV. He sat with his fingers in the juice while he flipped through channel after channel of morning news programs and talk shows. It wasn't the hosts that caught his attention though, it was the audience members. Everyone looked so happy together. Alexander turned his spongey neck from side to side and looked at the empty living room furniture. He looked at the spots where, the night before, Ms. Vanessa and Tara sat and joked around. He looked over at the recliner chair that still had one of Taylor's old hoodies tossed over the back of it. Just hours before, they were all together. But now, Alexander was by himself, and he didn't like it. *Is this loneliness?* Alexander wondered, this time internally.

Finding himself slowly growing sick of sitting alone in the living room, Alexander began exploring the apartment. Eventually, he found himself back in the kitchen and staring at the clock. It showed numbers that he didn't quite understand. That was irrelevant though, as the only numbers that mattered to him at this moment were 3:30. Alexander debated moving the microwave into the living room so that he could look at the clock while watching TV. He put his damp hands around it and tried to lift it up, but it slid through his weak grasp. He looked closely at where his hands had touched the microwave; he had accidentally washed away years of dust that had accumulated along the sides of the appliance.

◆ ◆ ◆

"So… How did things go with Alexander?" Mischa nervously asked as soon as Taylor stepped out of the apartment building.

"Much better than expected," Taylor replied as she passed Mischa a plastic travel mug full of coffee. It was scuffed up and clearly well-used; unbeknownst to Taylor, her sister and Tara had purchased it several years prior during a road trip to Seattle. Mischa's dad didn't allow her to drink coffee at home; unlike Taylor, Mischa's dad felt that she shouldn't do anything that could stunt her growth.

"That's good…" Mischa trailed off, waiting for Taylor to say something. Anything. Usually, Mischa stared at the ground while they walked to school together, but this morning she kept staring up at Taylor, hanging on every word.

"Don't worry Meesh, I'll tell you everything," Taylor said with a massive smile washing over her face. It was nice to have someone eager to listen to her. "Hey, after school, I need to take Alex shopping for some normal clothes. Do you want to come with me?"

"Absolutely," Mischa blurted out. "I mean, I need to pick up my last cheque from work anyway, so that sounds perfect," Mischa replied, struggling to sound calm and nonchalant, and not as if she was internally freaking out that her best friend's Grow a Friend toy had literally come to life.

Chapter Twelve

The moment right before the school bell rang at 3:00PM on Fridays was a magical time at Kelowna Secondary School. With rooms full of students apprehensively watching the clock and waiting for classes to be dismissed, and teachers having mostly given up on expecting their students to listen, the halls were as silent as a monastery at 2:59PM. As soon as the bell blared, though, the building's halls transitioned from being eerily silent to full of yells and chatter. Teens funneled out of the classrooms and packed around one another's lockers, all frantically confirming plans for the weekend. Wild talk of where the big party was happening, or who was going on a date with whom echoed throughout the otherwise boring off-white halls.

The majority of the younger students left the halls first, rushing to catch their buses home, while the older students tended to linger around talking, or blasting music from their cars in the parking lot. Taylor was happy that she walked home and therefore didn't need to rush to catch a bus and miss all of the action. She loved the bustle – the energy – of all of the older students. The way they carried themselves with a confidence that she didn't yet have. Mischa's focus was on Benjamin though. She watched from afar as the awkward teen lugged his massive baritone saxophone case towards his parents' minivan. In that moment, she wanted nothing more than for him to notice her. He hadn't tried talking to her in science class this morning, which made her worried that she had misread their previous interaction. *Maybe he didn't like her after all?* Mischa took her Lip Smackers out of her backpack and applied it with the confidence and deliberation of a model applying red lipstick before a photoshoot.

"How do I look?" Mischa asked, making a pout at Taylor.

"Great. Why are you asking though?" Taylor replied, confused. Her focus was on Lauren, the bully from gym class, whom she spotted hanging off of the arm of a much older male student. Taylor didn't notice Mischa walk away. The way that Lauren flipped her dyed hair as she laughed at the guy's every word was strangely hypnotic. She had the presence of a magnet. Cold and repelling to some, and extremely attractive to others. It wasn't that Taylor wanted to be friends with Lauren; she wanted to be her. Or be somewhat like her. She wanted to have that sort of charm and confidence that caused people to gravitate to her. Objectively, Taylor knew that Lauren was mean and not a great person, which is what made her magnetism even more confusing. Taylor knew that she shouldn't admire the mean kid at school, and yet she couldn't help it.

"Hey, I didn't know you were in band class?" Mischa asked rhetorically as she approached Benjamin. That was a lie though; seeing as eighth graders only got to pick two elective classes, they all had more or less the same schedule.

"Yeah, I just got picked for second chair today," Benjamin replied, slightly winded as he wiped a bead of sweat off of his forehead. Baritone saxophone cases were notoriously heavy to lug around. Mischa stared blankly, trying to think of the right thing to say.

"Second chair means that I play the supporting saxophone notes… If that makes sense…" Benjamin replied, sensing that Mischa had no idea what he was talking about.

"Oh, that's really cool," Mischa replied, "congrats." She tried her best to come across as chill and nonchalant, but hadn't planned anything to say past her opening line. Not being prepared stressed her out.

"There was only one other baritone player, so it's kind of like coming in last place," Benjamin faltered.

Struggling to think of a way to add to the conversation, Mischa decided to change the topic. "Hey so, I'm going to the mall with some friends tonight. Did you want to come with us?" she blurted out. She hadn't intended to ask him out, only to make conversation so that Benjamin would acknowledge her existence, but here they were… Mischa was in too deep now. Deep down, she really wasn't sure if she should invite him to tag along with Taylor and Alexander, since she wasn't sure if Alexander's existence was public knowledge or not, but she really couldn't think of anything else to invite Benjamin to.

"Are you asking me out?" Benjamin asked as he struggled to open the heavy back door of his parents' dark red Dodge

Caravan. He hoped that Mischa would assume his cheeks had grown darker from lugging the saxophone case, and not because he was blushing.

"Honey! Did you make a friend?" Benjamin's mom enthused from the drivers' seat as he ignored her and closed the door.

"I guess I am?" Mischa replied, surprising even herself with her confidence. It took every ounce of her strength not to push her bangs over her face and hide.

Benjamin paused. He could feel his entire body get warm. God, he hated how easily he blushed. He felt his stomach quickly twist into knots as he realized that his parents were taking him out of town this weekend. "I just remembered that I need to visit my grandparents then, but what about in a week or two? Maybe we could go to the Flintstones Park?"

"That sounds perfect," Mischa said, with a giant smile washing over her face. "Well, I uh, I'll see you in class on Monday then. I've got to go!" Having reached the limits of her confidence, Mischa turned away and hurried back to Taylor. If she had looked back over her shoulder, she would have noticed Benjamin looking back at her and smiling as he got into the van with his mom.

"What was that about?" Taylor asked, having missed Mischa's big moment.

"I did it," Mischa stated proudly.

"Did what?" Taylor asked.

"I asked a guy out."

"Damn," Taylor said while giving Mischa an enthusiastic high five. In that moment, Taylor had never admired someone's courage as much as she did with Mischa. She couldn't understand how everyone but her seemed so sure of themselves, but she knew this was something that she was going to have to work on. Suddenly, Taylor heard a familiar voice.

"Hey kiddos, get in!" Tara called out from behind the wheel of Big Blue. Her giant old truck rumbled so loudly that several people began to stare. Taylor hated it when she thought people were looking at her; she would have to work on her confidence another time.

"Is that... Alexander?" Mischa asked as she squinted into the distance. Seated next to Tara was a slight figure wearing an oversized hoodie and sunglasses. The sun was directly behind the truck, which made it hard to see.

"I think so?" Taylor replied. She became certain when the blurry figure waved back excitedly.

"Princess Taylor! I'm in a truck! Just like Mad Max!" The blurry outline of Alexander hollered enthusiastically.

The disguised sponge prince slid across the Ford Ranger's tweed bench seats and squished up against Tara as Taylor and Mischa hopped in.

"Where's Vanessa?" Taylor asked.

Tara paused a moment before bluntly answering, "She didn't want to ride in the back of the truck, so she stayed home." Finally beginning to accept and understand Tara's sarcasm, Taylor realized her question was silly. With four of them packed into Big Blue, there was definitely no room for a fifth person. She let out a small laugh. Tara smiled, silently proud of how well her and Taylor's relationship had grown over the past month.

"Why are you guys here?" Mischa asked. "I mean, don't get me wrong, I'm happy about the ride, I just assumed we'd have to walk…"

"I got off work early, and then realized that Alex couldn't very well go shopping in his all-green Jack and the Beanstalk ensemble, so I lent him some of my clothes and your hoodie that was left in the living room, I hope that's okay—" Tara explained.

"—It's not a problem at all," Taylor replied. She meant that. Somehow, the hoodie actually suited Alexander better than it did herself. The chunky teal and purple design helped to hide some of Alexander's excess moisture, which in a less conspicuous outfit, would make him appear as if he had just finished running a marathon.

"Tara was kind enough to offer to drop us off when I explained that walking to the mall in the sun might be too… dehydrating," Alexander explained as he picked up a large Nalgene water bottle off of the floor, and took a big drink. Taylor watched in amazement as he drank. "Oh! I found out I can use my mouth after all! My hands suck up liquid faster, but Tara suggested that I try drinking through my mouth in public, so I don't 'freak people out'," Alexander explained with air quotes. "Remind me later to show you what happens when I drink coloured sodas!"

Mischa continued to silently take everything in. The last time she had seen Alexander, he was threatening her with a sword, so she needed some time to absorb things.

"Look at us, a bunch of friends in a truck, driving through a city... Isn't life incredible?" Alexander mused as they turned down Springfield Road and made their way to the Orchard Park Mall. *It really is,* everyone inside the truck thought silently to themselves as their new sponge-based friend stared out the window, careful not to miss a single sight.

Chapter Thirteen

Having not stepped foot in the mall since about two weeks before school started, Taylor couldn't believe how busy it was on a Friday evening. If Kelowna Secondary School was an aquarium where everyone was forced to follow school rules, then the Orchard Park Mall was a coral reef where the bold and audacious finally got to show off.

"Wow," Alexander exclaimed as a group of kids with neon hair darted by like tetra fish. Taylor didn't say anything, but she related to Alexander's sense of awe. In fact, she pretty much *was* him only a few months ago. It was nice to be able to see a bit of herself reflected in Alexander, as it wasn't often that Taylor was able to relate to people.

"Are you guys cool with me leaving to pick up my last pay cheque from work?" Mischa asked.

Taylor hesitated to say yes, as the size of the mall still scared her a little, but she knew she would be okay until Mischa returned. "Okay. Let's meet up in the food court in thirty minutes?"

"Sounds good," Mischa said with a combination nod slash hair flip, and she headed off towards her old workplace. With Mischa gone, Taylor wasn't really sure where to take Alexander first.

"So… What sort of clothes do you think you want?" Taylor asked him, while scanning the sea of shoppers.

"I don't know," Alexander responded sincerely. "What—*who*," Alexander corrected himself, "Who do you think I should be?"

Taylor struggled to think of the right thing to say, but managed the best she could. "Clothes are not about who you want to be, it's about expressing who you are." *Wow, did I come up with those words myself?* she wondered to herself.

"I guess I don't know who I am yet," Alexander spoke softly. His British accent cracked slightly, causing him to take a sip from his giant water bottle. "But I think I like those clothes?" he said, pointing to a simply dressed middle-aged man who was working at San Francisco Gifts. Taylor paused as she realized that the man was the sales clerk who sold her Alexander. A sinking feeling swelled up inside of her gut. It was as if she was both extremely full, and nauseous at the same time.

"Are you okay, Princess Taylor?" Alexander asked.

"I'm… I'm fine," Taylor paused to clear her throat. Alexander passed her his bottle of water, which she graciously accepted.

"Why did that upset you? Should I not like those clothes?" Alexander asked, as Taylor tried to get her anxiety under control.

◆ ◆ ◆

Ah, yes. My first job, Mischa thought to herself with a misplaced sense of nostalgia as she stepped into Mariposa, the clothing store that she had spent the summer working at. It had only been two weeks since she quit working to return to school, but to Mischa, it felt like a million years. She peered through her black bangs and examined the new clothes that were on display. *They get ready for winter earlier every year,* she thought, as she gave a distasteful look to the polar fleece coats that had recently been put on display. Yuck. If it were up to her, everything furry or fluffy would be burnt in a dumpster fire.

"Hi, I'm here to pick up my pay cheque?" Mischa asked the new girl that was working at the cash register.

"Um, like who are you?" the wide-eyed sales clerk asked. Mischa glanced at her name tag: Staci. The i was dotted with a heart sticker.

"Up until two weeks ago, I was you," Mischa said, much to the confusion of the sales clerk. "I mean, I used to have your job." Staci with an i still didn't understand.

"I'm just gonna get my manager," Staci replied flippantly.

"Oh hey, Meesh," a large middle-aged woman crooned. Her voice was soft, but was clearly hiding something.

"Hi Sandy," Mischa replied, her forehead furrowed with unease. Unbeknownst to most, Mischa's face was quite expressive, you just couldn't tell from behind her thick fringe.

"Here's your last cheque, thanks-for-coming, okay-I've-got-to-go—" Sandy spoke in rapid succession as she passed, or more aptly, threw an envelope at Mischa as she turned to run and hide back in the stock room.

"Uh, is something wrong?" Mischa asked while ripping the envelope open and pulling out her final paystub.

Hours Worked: 45 hours
Gross Total: $270
Special Deductions: -$120
Net Total: $150

"Sandy, come back here—" Mischa called out, causing Sandy to stop in her tracks. "Where's the other half of my pay? What are these 'special deductions?' This has to be a mistake."

"Mischa, when you started working here, I was blown away by how much you were selling. Literally blown away. You sold more than any worker I've ever had—"

"But?" Mischa pressed. She was not letting this go.

"But, over half of what you sold got returned! You somehow charmed everyone into buying things that they didn't really want or that didn't even fit them. We have had so many returns since you stopped working here, that I had to take a deduction from your pay cheque. I'm sorry. I really am," Sandy stammered as the rosacea on her cheeks started to flare up. She was clearly not good with confrontations and had worked herself into a sweaty and flustered mess.

"You took half my pay?" Mischa asked in disbelief. "I need this last cheque. I worked hard all summer, and this is my thanks?"

"Be thankful you got anything," Sandy muttered while once again beginning to walk away.

"This isn't legal," Mischa said, trying her best to keep from getting upset.

"Yeah, but what can you do?" Mischa's sweaty ex-manager said dismissively while closing the stock door behind her. Earlier in the summer, one employee found an empty Snickers box underneath a stack of jeans. While there was no proof that Sandy always offered to "work on stock" because she was secretly eating candy, the evidence was pretty damning – especially in the afternoons when Sandy's blood sugar would start to drop and she'd disappear to nap in her car.

Knowing that she was out of options, Mischa tucked the pay cheque in her black backpack, and turned to leave the store. "Have a great day!" the misnamed Stacey said with a perverted sense of glee. At least, that's how Mischa interpreted her words, so as a final act of retribution, Mischa pushed over the giant display of polar fleece coats as she left the store.

"You too!" Mischa yelled back, mimicking the sales clerk's overly-sweet tone. Realizing that she may have accidentally just committed a crime, Mischa speed-walked away from the clothing store as quickly as she could, and decided to hide out in the washrooms until the heat blew over.

Taylor sat quietly on one of the mall benches as she struggled to find the words to explain things to Alexander. How was she supposed to tell him that she bought him on sale from the very store he now wanted to shop in? He stared with apprehension, as Taylor fidgeted by repeatedly pressing the backlight button on her watch.

"Alex, I don't know how to explain things, I just..." Taylor mumbled.

"Princess Taylor, I don't want to interrupt you, but are you nervous to tell me that you bought me from that store?" Alexander interjected in his usual high octave tone.

Taylor wasn't sure how to respond. *How did he know that? Oh God, can Alexander also read minds?*

"And before you ask, no I cannot read minds," Alexander replied with a laugh. Taylor stared at him, now a little freaked out.

"Then how do you know that's where you're from?" Taylor asked. Unlike Mischa, her face was not as expressive. Sure, she could raise her eyebrows but for the most part Taylor's expressions were pretty static. She couldn't even wink; it was something the entire Gagnon family struggled with. Vanessa used to joke that they were like a family of washed-up soap actors.

"Well, Princess Taylor, the posters that are displayed at the store match the commercials that play all day on TV," Alexander said with a shrug. "I know that I came from a plastic egg, and that I am not real. I am just a Grow a Friend T. M."

Hearing Alexander say the words "not real" stung Taylor's heart. It was in that moment that she knew he was very much real. Human, no, but real nonetheless. "Of course you're real," Taylor said, placing her hand on Alexander's damp shoulder. "Just because you were brought into this world differently, does not mean you're not real." The disguised-sponge prince paused, and took this in. He held out his hand next to Taylor's. His was smooth and printless, and slightly soggier, but it was clearly a real hand.

"We don't need to go in the store," Taylor explained. "They don't even sell the clothes that that man is wearing."

"I still want to go in. I want to feel brave," Alexander said as he got to his feet. "After all, I am supposed to be royalty." Taylor noticed the small pool of water that he left behind on the bench, and tried her best to discretely wipe it off with her sleeve before someone noticed.

Chapter Fourteen

Having successfully evaded mall security, which wasn't much of a challenge if she was being honest, Mischa found herself emotionally trapped in the women's washroom. She knew that by now she had gotten away scot-free after knocking over the rack of clothes at her old place of work, but she couldn't bring herself to leave. She was just so… angry. Angry, hurt, and unable to express it appropriately in this moment. Her face was hot with rage. She wanted to break something, or scream, but was unable to do either. Everyone – her dad, teachers, brother Michael – everyone was always telling her to focus. Well, now she was focused and she couldn't stand it. Mischa wished that she could stop thinking about how her stupid boss ripped her off. The washroom offered a sense of solace, as it was the only place in the mall that she could be alone. Mischa turned on the sink and splashed cold water on her face. Unfortunately, that made her mascara run. *Great, now I look like a sad raccoon,* Mischa thought to herself as she grabbed a piece of paper towel and attempted to fix her mistake.

"Bleeeehhhhggh!"

What was that? Mischa thought to herself as she realized that she wasn't alone. The awful vomiting noise was followed by the flush of a toilet. Another burst of "Bleeerrrrghh" came from the washroom stall, several sinks away. Mischa paused, unsure of what to do. She wanted a distraction, but this wasn't quite what she had in mind.

"Are… Are you okay in there?" Mischa called out, her anger now changing to a feeling of concern.

Several slow seconds later, a weak voice bluntly called out, "I'm fine." Mischa stared for a moment as her least favourite person, Lauren, exited the stall. The two girls looked at each other like two beta fish sizing each other up in a small aquarium, debating if they should fight or flee.

"Oh. It's you," Lauren muttered. "Don't say anything to anyone," she said while haphazardly fixing her hair in the washroom mirror and walking away.

Mischa couldn't help but continue to stare at Lauren throughout the entirety of their interaction. It was like she just discovered how they got the caramel into Caramilk bars. *Taylor isn't going to believe this.*

Lauren wasn't sure what to think as she exited the washroom. Embarrassment, shame, anger… Her heart felt like it was going to beat right out of her chest. So many feelings washed over her as she stood just outside of the washroom door. She hoped and prayed that Mischa wouldn't follow her and would give her a few minutes to collect herself. Of all of the people in the world, why did it have to be Mischa that discovered her secret? As someone with a deep interest in astrology, though, it sort of made sense. *It had to be Mischa,* Lauren rationalized to herself, *this is karma.*

When she wasn't competing on multiple sports teams or hanging out with the guys, Lauren was nose deep in books on astrology and manifesting your best life. As a teenager with controlling parents and very little agency in her own life, astrology gave Lauren a sense of ease. When things got too tough and life spiraled out of control, she found it comforting to read about which planets were in retrograde. It wasn't her fault that her parents screamed at her, or that her boyfriend called her fat when she experimented with a new outfit, it was because *Mercury was too close to the Moon,* or whatever. And now, because of all of the cruel things that Lauren had said to or about Mischa and her brother Michael, the universe was punishing her by having Mischa know about her secret struggle with food. This realization disturbed Lauren, because she realized she was probably eventually going to have to start treating Mischa nicer in class, but... Lauren sighed. She just found the little twerp so annoying. Mischa was everything she wasn't: smart, witty, and oddly self-assured. How was Lauren ever supposed to compete with that? Just as Lauren's pulse returned to normal, she heard the washroom door begin to squeak open, so she hurried away as quickly as she could. True to Lauren's Libra nature, she just couldn't bear another run in with Mischa right now.

Taylor took Alexander's hand and gripped it reassuringly as they stood outside of the San Francisco Gifts store. The giant neon sign flickered slightly, clearly nearing the end of its life. Taylor glanced at the spinner racks of knickknacks that stood on either side of the store's entrance like extremely underwhelming pillars. Then, right there, along the side wall, she spotted it: the recently built Grow a Friend display.

"Are you sure you want to go in?" Taylor once again asked Alexander. Alexander nodded, before leading the way and walking directly to the sales clerk.

"Excuse me, sir," Alexander squeaked. "I would like to enquire about your Grow a Friend toys?"

"Can't you read, kid? The sign says the toys aren't being sold for another month—" the sales clerk retorted as he spun around from the rack of snow globes that he was in the middle of re-pricing. "Oh hey, it's you," he said, his voice softening, when he realized that he recognized Taylor. His tone soured again though, as he looked back at Alexander. "I told you I was doing you a favour! Now you're bringing friends here too?" the clerk continued exasperatedly. "I've been skating on thin ice here since I accidentally dropped a box of lava lamps."

"I- I'm sorry," Taylor replied.

"It's not her fault," Alexander rebutted, "I asked to come here."

"Look, I can't sell you any Grow a Friends, kid. Not until corporate says I can," the clerk shot back, while turning to acknowledge two window-shoppers who just exited the elusive backroom.

Alexander looked to Taylor permissively. Taylor shrugged. "I don't want to buy a Grow a Friend, I just have some questions," Alexander pushed, clearly mimicking someone from another TV show. The clerk sighed before setting his pricing gun down and resigning himself to the fact that he was going to have to listen to these two random teenagers. *What is it?* the clerk seemed to ask non-verbally, by placing his hand on his hip.

"Where do the toys come from?" Alexander asked.

"China," the clerk answered bluntly.

"From a family?" Alexander pressed.

"No, a factory!" the clerk retorted, now wondering if this kid he was talking to was okay.

"Are they treated well?" Alexander asked.

"What do you mean? We get boxes of them, and then they sit here until they're ready to sell," the clerk stated. "They're not free range like chickens if that's what you're wondering." *Is this kid for real?* he thought to himself.

"Okay, that's all, thank you," Alexander replied.

"Ugh, fine, you broke me," the clerk said with a groan, as he reached under the counter and pulled out another damaged Grow a Friend egg. "You can buy this little guy for $10, if you'd like. He's marked down extra because I once again slipped with the box cutter—"

Taylor and Alexander looked down at the little plastic egg that was sitting on the counter. Alexander picked it up, and cracked it open in the palm of his hand: out fell a little Grow a Friend puppy with a disproportionately stubby tail. Alexander looked to Taylor. Without saying a word to each other, Taylor knew exactly what he wanted her to do. She reached into her wallet, and pulled out a $10 bill which she exchanged for the Grow a Friend. "Now please get out of here, before my boss finds out I sold you another one of these toys," the wildly inconsistent and clumsy clerk insisted.

As the two of them left San Francisco Gifts, plastic egg safely nestled in Alexander's hoodie pocket, Taylor couldn't help but wonder how many Grow a Friends toys that sales clerk had already sold.

"So, he just sold you another one, for ten dollars?" Mischa asked while staring at the stubby-tailed Grow a Friend pup that was placed in the centre of the food court table. "I thought these toys—" Mischa corrected herself as she made eye contact with Alexander, "that these... beings? I thought that they were supposed to be super exclusive?" Alexander reached into the middle of the table and carefully put the miniature dehydrated dog back into its plastic egg, which he continued to hold protectively. "I'm sorry, Alex, I didn't mean to call you a toy..." Mischa said solemnly.

"It isn't inaccurate," Alexander said with a shrug. The usually chipper prince was clearly in a funk.

"You're not a toy," Taylor piped up. "I mean, you technically were at one point—" she rambled, "but you aren't now. You're as real as either of us."

"How do you know that though?" Alexander asked, as if he genuinely expected either of the young girls to know.

"We just do. Sometimes, a gut feeling is all you need," Taylor said earnestly, while Mischa pulled out a small make-up mirror from her backpack. Mischa got up, and sat back down on the empty chair that was between Taylor and Alex. She flipped open the mirror, and held it up for Alexander to see.

"I'm not a scientist, but I know when I look in this mirror, I don't see a toy," Mischa spoke, "I see three friends." It took all of her strength, but Mischa managed to be sincere without cringing.

"Thank you," Alexander said softly, as he put his damp arms around the two friends and pulled them in for a hug. "Mischa, I am sorry I called you a wench."

"Apology accepted," Mischa said, trying her best to ignore the water that squished from Alexander's arm during his embrace. During the touching moment, Mischa overheard the whirring sounds of the blenders from Orange Julius and immediately got a craving for one. "Who else wants something from Orange Julius?" Having already understood that Mischa was easily distracted, neither Taylor nor Alexander thought it was strange for her to blurt that out.

As Mischa left to buy them drinks, Alexander once again cracked open the container of his Grow a Friend pup.

"Are you going to put him in water?" Taylor asked. She wanted to explain that they should probably consult with Vanessa and Tara first, since a dog was a lot of responsibility, but thought better of bringing that up in the moment.

"Do you think he will come to life like I did?" Alexander asked while staring at the loonie-sized dog.

"I don't know," Taylor replied. She really didn't know. Maybe Alexander was entirely unique. There was no way of knowing until all of the Grow a Friend toys were officially for sale and released into the world. "It's worth a shot though?"

"I'm not sure if I should have a dog right now, there is so much that I still need to figure out," Alexander pondered aloud. Taylor nodded in a way that she hoped would be interpreted as supportive, and not as if she was telling him what to do. Alexander had a lot on his extremely young plate, and she didn't want to add to his worries.

In this moment, it felt as if Taylor was living in an After School Special. None of those TV shows ever dealt with things like existentialism though; all Taylor had learned from those episodes was how to say no if the popular kid offered you drugs. Looking over at Mischa awkwardly trying to flirt with one of the greasy boys at the Orange Julius counter, and then at the incredibly damp Alexander who had by now soaked through his hoodie, Taylor accepted that none of them were going to need to decline party invitations from dangerous cool kids anytime soon.

Chapter Fifteen

There was nothing quite as pathetic as a Monday morning gym class. Although the class was only an hour and a half long, it might as well have been a prison sentence to the sweaty and out of shape teenagers who'd have preferred to still be in bed, or heck, even math class. Groggy teens tried their best not to slip on the dewy school field as they struggled to complete their weekly circuit training. Because of the time of day, the sun would shine directly into the eyes of the students as they ran across the field. The problem could have been fixed if they just ran back and forth across the field horizontally instead of doing laps, but that would shorten the total distance by several metres and therefore not be "regulation" so everyone went along with it. Taylor couldn't understand why the gym coach couldn't just add another lap to make up for it, but she didn't want to engage in a conversation with him. The smart students wore sunglasses to block out the blinding early morning rays that shone directly across the field, but Taylor and Mischa were not amongst those students.

The two friends finished running a lap around the field, talking in-between gasps of air, before haphazardly struggling through their government mandated round of ten burpees. The supportive-but-incredibly-annoying coach hollered instructions from the sidelines. Neither Taylor nor Mischa knew who the instructions were for, as multiple students were on different stages of the circuit. The coach's tone was not unhappy, but no one liked to be yelled at on a Monday morning, even if the words were vague and encouraging.

"And up! And down! Come on guys, pick up your arms!"

Taylor and Mischa paused and looked at each other questioningly. *Pick up our arms?*

"Yeah, hurry up guys," Lauren snarked as she finished her burpees and sprinted off to complete her last lap. In what could only be considered a moment of luck, Mischa managed to lock eyes with her bully just long enough to make sure that Lauren saw her gagging gesture. Despite having spent all morning in gym class, Lauren's face turned a ghostly white as she immediately looked away from Mischa and sprinted off.

"What was that about?" Taylor asked, having never witnessed anything like that before.

"I'll tell you later," Mischa mumbled as the bell went off, signalling the end of class. It always sucked when gym class went late because the several minutes the students had between classes was hardly enough time to get cleaned up postworkout. The boys could soak themselves in pungent body spray, but the girls hardly had enough time to brush their hair let alone fix their make-up. Taylor brought this up to Vanessa and Tara once, but had to listen to Tara rant about something called the 'beauty myth' for the following hour, so for now she was going to keep her thoughts about the unfairness of post gym class esthetics to herself.

"Hey, it's two of my star cross-country runners!" the coach called to Taylor and Mischa as they left the change room. The girls both knew the compliment was hollow, as they hadn't even participated in cross-country yet – the most they had accomplished was signing up for it the previous week. "Don't forget that we have our first Milk Run in two weeks, up in Mission. Make sure you get your permission slips signed, since we're going to have to bus there."

"Okay, thank you," Taylor said as she accepted the yellow piece of copier paper and placed it in the back pocket of her jeans. She had no idea what a Milk Run was, but didn't want to come across as dumb by asking.

"Thanks, teach," Mischa said with a nod, while walking away and not actually taking the permission slip.

"Uh, I think you'll need that," Taylor spoke up.

"It's fine, I haven't returned a permission slip in years and no one has ever said anything," Mischa said nonchalantly.

"I trust you, but I really don't want to run this thing alone," Taylor said, with a hint of annoyance in her voice.

"Fine," Mischa scoffed as she turned around and accepted the permission slip from the coach, who was still standing there with the paper in his hand, "for you."

"Thank you," Taylor breathed a sigh of relief. She admired Mischa's confidence, but really didn't want either of them to get in trouble. "Meesh, I've got to ask—"

"—Are you wondering what the heck a Milk Run is?" Mischa interrupted.

"Yeah," Taylor replied.

"It's what it sounds like," Mischa offered. "They make us kids run, and then we get free milk afterwards." Noticing the confused look on Taylor's face, Mischa tried her best to explain things further, but fell short. "Honestly, it's not as weird as it sounds. I mean, when has free chocolate milk ever been a bad thing?" Taylor couldn't disagree with that.

Just as they approached their recently-sanitized lockers, something happened that might have been from one of the war movies that Taylor used to catch her dad watching late at night. A shell-shocked looking eighth grade student, coated head to toe in a white powder, flour most likely, came running around the hallway corner faster than anyone in Taylor's gym class could have managed.

"Rrrrruuuunnnnnnnn!" The boy yelled as if he was in slow motion. "Iiiitttttt'ssss Ggggrraaaaddeee Eeeiiiigggghhhhtttt Pppplllllaaaayyyy Ddddaaaayyyy!" the eighth grade Paul Revere cried out right as he slipped face first on the residual polish left over from the summer deep clean of the school, leaving a trail of flour in his wake as he slid across the floor. In that moment, Taylor finally understood the school's no running policy.

"We need to help him!" Taylor called out as Mischa grabbed her arm and pulled her back.

"It's too late, he's already gone," Mischa spoke with a hushed voice, as a group of eleventh graders dog-piled on the floury boy and began to duct tape him to the off-white concrete wall. Sensing that they may be next, and wanting no part of it, Taylor and Mischa grabbed their backpacks and hurried away from the horrible scene as quickly as they could. Just as they were about to exit through the front doors, Mischa spotted Benjamin, lugging his baritone saxophone out of the band class room. She grabbed his arm as she had with Taylor, and proceeded to pull him down the hallway with them.

"Uh, what's going on?" Benjamin asked, already winded after several seconds of running.

"Grade Eight Play Day," Mischa replied with utmost seriousness.

"Oh no," Benjamin replied solemnly.

"Why is there never anything good on during the day?" Tara complained while Vanessa clicked through the same twenty TV channels. Every so often they had Mondays off together, which was lucky, because they realized that they really needed to spend more time with Alexander. While Vanessa and Tara didn't usually spend their free time watching television, he had insisted they all watch TV together while they ate lunch, like a real American family would. Alexander didn't understand that they lived in Canada, and as Tara had conceded, it didn't really matter. After lunch, the plan was to visit the library and maybe a park; Vanessa and Tara were both a little concerned at how much TV was influencing Alexander and wanted him to become a more well-rounded person.

"Why is everyone so angry?" Alexander asked inquisitively as Vanessa settled on watching The Jerry Springer Show.

"Nes, really?" Tara asked in an uncharacteristically non-sarcastic way. "Alex is just a kid." Vanessa looked over at her new impressionable sponge friend. Sibling? Adopted son? She wasn't really sure what their relationship was at this point, but couldn't dispute Tara's disapproval that having him watch The Jerry Springer Show probably wasn't appropriate.

"Good point," Vanessa said as she continued clicking through the channels.

"But I wanted to see what the bead necklaces were for!" Alexander called out. "Vanessa, can we buy beads today?" he asked with wide-eyed sincerity.

"Uh, sure little dude," Vanessa offered, much to Alexander's joy. Alexander clapped his hands together in celebration, causing a fine mist to spray from his palms.

"Do either of you want more nachos?" Tara asked while standing up to bring their plates to the kitchen. The question was mostly directed at Vanessa, since Alexander didn't need to eat, but it felt rude to exclude him. While he didn't need to consume any calories, he seemed to enjoy holding the plates of food and being a part of family meals.

Just as everyone passed their plates to Tara, there was a knock at the door, followed by someone calling out "Knock, knock!" as the door creaked open.

Tara and Vanessa locked eyes with each other in panic, while Alexander remained on the couch, confused. "Alex, I really hate to do this to you, but could you go and hang out in Taylor's room for a while?" Vanessa whispered.

"There's no time!" Tara whisper-yelled, as she flung the blanket that was hanging over the back of the couch over top of Alex. He had no idea what was happening, and wasn't sure why people kept trying to hide him under blankets, but figured now wasn't the time to ask questions.

Vanessa jumped up, and tried to greet her parents at the front door before they were able to make it into the living room. It was a small apartment, so she had to move fast. "Hey Mom… Dad…?" Vanessa said with a confused tone. "What are you doing here?"

"What are we doing here? That's a rude way to greet your mom and I after you haven't seen us in months," Mr. Gagnon retorted.

"I think it's been closer to two years," Vanessa mumbled.

"Well, give us a hug!" Mrs. Gagnon said while leaning in and giving Vanessa a very awkward and very unwanted hug. Mid-embrace, she spotted Tara who was standing just around the corner. "Oh, hello again," Mrs. Gagnon mused, "Vanessa, why is the odd neighbour girl here?" she said while lowering her voice to a hush.

"Why are you here?" Vanessa repeated, while stepping away from Mr. and Mrs. Gagnon. Tara stood awkwardly behind her, unsure of how to handle the situation. She wanted to support Vanessa, but knew of the terrible history with her family and didn't want to cause a yelling match. It would be easier for everyone if the Gagnons would just leave without incident.

"We're here to see Taylor," Mr. Gagnon offered. "We both got a little bored and thought, hey, let's go visit our girls in the big city. Plus, I need to pick up the suitcases Taylor took with her when she moved here."

"Your father and I are planning a vacation!" Mrs. Gagnon blurted out untactfully.

There it was, the real reason they were here, Vanessa suddenly realized. "You haven't seen me in years, or Taylor in weeks, and you decide to stop by unannounced just to pick up some old suitcases you *graciously* let her borrow?" Vanessa said, her face beginning to feel hot.

Alexander really wanted to say something from underneath his crocheted hiding place, but continued to use all of his efforts to remain hidden.

"It's a Monday afternoon. Why would you even assume that Taylor would be home?" Tara said, unable to keep biting her tongue.

"Does someone want to tell me why the neighbour girl is involved in this conversation?" Mrs. Gagnon said bluntly.

"You know exactly why she's here," Vanessa offered, trying her best to remain calm. Before Taylor moved in, she would have continued to lie about Tara's existence just to keep the peace. Now that she had her little sister to look after, and Alexander, Vanessa knew that she needed to set an example.

"La la la la, I don't want to hear it!" Mr. Gagnon said while plugging his ears. Tara looked to Vanessa, wondering if they were really going to have this conversation with her parents right now, and also wondering if her eyes were deceiving her or if there really was a grown man acting like a small child in their kitchen.

"Vanessa! You know we don't talk about those sorts of things in our household!" Mrs. Gagnon said in a hushed whisper that was all too familiar to anyone that grew up in the Gagnon family.

"That's why I left in the first place," Vanessa said, the redness of her face further emphasized against her blonde hair. "And this is our household, not yours," she continued as Tara stepped forward and wrapped her arm supportively around Vanessa's waist.

"All we wanted to do was see our good daughter and get my suitcase back, was that too much to ask?" Mr. Gagnon said with the indignity of someone with extremely limited self-awareness. Mrs. Gagnon stood quietly with her hand dramatically on her forehead. Feeling faint was her go-to move to get out of uncomfortable conversations, but Vanessa wasn't going to fall for it.

"Mom, Dad, this is my girlfriend, Tara. We are very much in love and have been for roughly a decade. If you can't accept that I'm gay after all of these years, that's your problem and not mine," Vanessa announced. Just as the redness from Vanessa's face began to fade, Alexander emerged from around the corner of the kitchen wearing the blanket like a cape.

"Mom, Dad... Don't listen to her! They just trying to protect me, I am Vanessa's real boyfriend!" Alexander proclaimed, having clearly been influenced by the episodes of Jerry Springer that he had watched in secret.

"Alex, what are you doing?" Tara asked through the side of her mouth.

"I am causing a scene, so that they get mad at me instead of you!" Alex loudly whispered to Tara.

"Who the H-E-double hockey sticks in this?" Mrs. Gagnon asked.

"Vanessa, why is there a small British boy living with you? Do you have a secret kid too? What else are you keeping from us?" Mr. Gagnon accused.

"I am Prince Alexander Charming, and I am here to protect my family from intruders like you! Begone!" Alexander demanded, while dramatically throwing off his now-soaked blanket cape which landed with a wet thud.

"Alex, you don't need to do this," Vanessa said kindly as she placed her hand on his shoulder. "Mom, Dad, let's try this again. I'm gay. You know this. In fact, it's why I left home at sixteen, or rather, was forced to. Do you remember that? Do you remember how you constantly insulted me at every chance? Called me an abomination? Well, guess what, I'm definitely still a lesbian. This is Tara and she is my girlfriend, not some neighbour. I am embarrassed that I had her lie to you about that in the first place." By now, Alexander was standing between Tara and Vanessa, who were guarding him as parents would. "This little guy here is correct, his name really is Prince

Alexander Charming. But he is definitely not my boyfriend and was just trying to protect me. He's family, and that's honestly all of the explanation you deserve."

"How rude," Mrs. Gagnon said without batting an eye.

"I'm grabbing the suitcases, and then we're leaving," Mr. Gagnon mumbled.

Tara grabbed the suitcases from Taylor's room, passed them to Mr. Gagnon, and then locked the door as soon as the couple left. Vanessa overheard her mother complaining "They didn't even ask about our vacation plans," as they shuffled down the apartment hallway, and was extremely relieved to no longer have them in her life.

"I am so happy that you guys are my real family," Vanessa said, as she pulled Tara and Alexander close for a hug. She wasn't sure if she should ever tell Taylor about what happened with their parents on that day, but was grateful that she was Taylor's guardian now and that her little sister was free from those bigots from Craigellachie.

Chapter Sixteen

Sweaty, winded, and several blocks from Kelowna Secondary School, Taylor, Mischa, and Benjamin found themselves standing in a gas station parking lot. "I don't think I've ever ran that far in my life," Benjamin gasped as he retrieved an inhaler from his backpack, internally thankful to have left his heavy saxophone back at school. His mom had ironed his buttoned-up shirt for him that morning, but now you could no longer tell. The three Grade Eight Play Day escapees were so winded and dishevelled it looked as if they had escaped from Alcatraz. Gasping as she caught her reflection in the gas station window, Mischa pulled out a small hair brush from her backpack and began to fix her hair.

"What should we do now?" Taylor asked to both no one and everyone as she paced around the parking lot. She had never skipped school before, but after seeing her flour-coated classmate get tackled in the hallway, she figured it was understandable to play hooky today.

"I could call my mom and get her to drive us somewhere?" Benjamin offered. "Although she'd probably ground me for skipping class…"

"Even though you'd end up duct-taped to a wall if you stayed behind?" Mischa asked, perturbed.

"My family really values education," Benjamin replied with a shrug.

Looking through her wallet, Taylor noticed she had a couple of extra dollars. "How much does a taxi cost?" she asked Mischa.

"How should I know, I've never taken one before," Mischa responded while looking through her bright neon green coin purse. It was the only brightly coloured thing she owned, and if anyone asked it was because she was being ironic. The truth was, though, that Mischa secretly loved lime green. "I've got an extra twenty bucks though. How far do you think that would get us?"

"Let's ask," Benjamin said as he approached a taxi that was filling up at the gas pump. "Excuse me," he asked nervously as the taxi driver filled up the car. "How much would it cost to go to the Flintstones Park?"

"Flintstones park? That old place?" The taxi driver replied while eyeing up the three tired looking teenagers. "I could take you there for five bucks. Why aren't you in class though?"

"It's Grade Eight Play Day," Benjamin replied with a seriousness to his voice well beyond his thirteen years.

"Say no more," the taxi driver replied, clearly remembering the traumatic experience from his own high school days. "Hop in," the kind hearted taxi driver called out to Taylor and Mischa. "I'll take you there for free. I need to head out that way anyhow."

Only ten minutes later, the taxi pulled up to the Flintstones-themed park, Bedrock City. "Here's my card," the taxi driver said as he passed his card to Benjamin. "You kids give me a call if you need a drive somewhere else, you know, if you get sick of this park after a few minutes."

"Thank you?" Benjamin replied, slightly embarrassed. It was his idea to come to the park after all, so he really didn't want it to suck. He had next to no experience hanging out with girls, other than his mom, and the last thing Benjamin wanted was to look like a loser in front of Mischa.

One by one the friends hopped out of the taxi and took notice of the behemoth in front of them. There he was... In all of his former glory: Forty Foot Fred. Forty Foot Fred was the moniker given to the giant wooden cut-out of Fred Flintstone that acted as the park billboard. Taylor wasn't sure how accurate the name was, and wondered if anyone had actually measured the billboard, but she could believe that he was least thirty feet, which was still impressive, she supposed.

"I haven't been here since I was five, so, um... My memory may be a little foggy," Benjamin replied while noticing the large pieces of paint that were peeling off of Fred, making the giant cartoon caveman look as if he had a skin condition.

"It's okay, we won't blame you if it sucks," Mischa offered, before realizing she might have been mean to the boy that she had only ever spoken to a handful of times before. "Old places can be cool too!"

"Why is it so empty?" Taylor asked as she peered around the mostly vacant parking lot.

"Monday morning isn't exactly prime theme park time I guess," Benjamin offered as he approached the ticket taker at the gate. The employee had their feet up on the counter, and a baseball hat over their face. "Excuse me... We'll take three—" Benjamin scanned the price board that was hung above the cave-shaped ticketing booth, "—youth tickets please," he said with a sense of pride as he realized that he was now considered a youth instead of a child, even though that meant paying more. The ticket taker let out an audible snore. "Ex-excuse me?" Benjamin asked.

"What are you doing? Don't wake him up," Mischa said while gently elbowing Benjamin. "This means we can get in for free!"

Were they really going to do it? Were they going to sneak into a theme park? They had already ditched school for the day – Taylor really wasn't comfortable with committing two crimes in the same morning, but here they were. She found herself holding her breath as they walked through the gates.

"You okay?" Mischa asked. "Come on, let's go," she said as she took Taylor's hand and pulled her into the park.

Bedrock City had definitely seen better days. The bumper cars were closed and there was no sign indicating if that was because it was a Monday morning, or if they were closed for repairs. The fake caves and stone walls that were scattered throughout the park seemed to suffer the same peeling-paint ailment that afflicted Forty Foot Fred, and the stone-aged themed boat ride had been closed off as well, leaving a slimy algae-lined pool that seemed to exist only to taunt children. The inactive boats seemed to call out, "Hey kids, look how much fun you *could* be having right now!"

"Is this where teenagers usually hang out?" Taylor asked, genuinely unsure. She was so used to being overwhelmed with the excitement of new experiences since moving to Kelowna, that she was taken back at how disappointing the park was.

"Well, they used to," Benjamin replied, his voice trailing off as he scanned the empty park. "Hey, look! There are other people here after all! See, I'm not a loser," he blurted out smugly as he spotted three other teens hanging out by the concession booth which was meant to look like a cave, but more closely resembled a split-open baked potato.

"No one called you a loser," Mischa offered with a tone of concern. Was her new crush really that insecure? She felt her dreams of the two of them becoming a world-famous power couple dashing away before they ever really began.

"Ice cream is on me," Taylor offered while hurrying towards the cave-shaped concession. She could sense an awkward feeling bubbling up between Mischa and Benjamin and wanted to get out of it as quickly as she could. She scanned the menu of stone-aged inspired desserts. "Uh, could I please get something in grape?" Taylor asked the unenthused concession worker. At least, she imagined that they were unenthusiastic;

they were wearing a giant fur costume in the shape of Dino, the pet dinosaur from the show.

"Hey, you're that girl from homeroom," Kai S-Something said as he spotted Taylor from the other side of the concession cave. Startled, Taylor's arms failed, causing her to almost drop her grape flavoured Flintstones branded Push Pop. "You okay, spaz?"

"Y-yeah. I'm fine," Taylor sputtered before clearing her throat. "I'm cool, everything is cool."

"Okay then," Kai said while looking off into the distance. The awkward silence hung in the air as Taylor struggled to think of something to say. What was he always thinking about? Or was Taylor just that boring? She rationalized that it was also possible that he had that Attention Deficit Disorder that they talked about a lot on talk shows, or maybe he was just a jerk. In any case, his aloofness made Taylor want to understand Kai even more.

"So, um, are you here with people?" Taylor stammered, realizing how dumb her question sounded.

"Yeah, I'm here with some friends. They had to use the pay phones so I'm just, like, waiting here for them to come back," Kai said before taking a bite of his ice cream sandwich. "One day, we'll totally have phones everywhere, so we won't need to waste quarters on payphones. And spaceships with racing stripes..." he continued on, as if he had already forgotten that Taylor was standing there.

"I... I am getting my own phone line in my bedroom," Taylor asserted.

"That's pretty cool," Kai replied, once again acknowledging his awkward admirer's presence. "Oh hey, it's my friends," he said again to no one in particular before turning to Taylor, "It was nice talking with you." Taylor froze in awe as her homeroom crush walked away and towards his two equally cool friends.

"Taylor?" Mischa said, while tapping Taylor on the shoulder. Miraculously, Taylor didn't jump. "Earth to Taylor?" Mischa said louder, while snapping her fingers.

"Oh, hey Meesh! I didn't see you," Taylor replied in a dazed tone.

"He's not *that* ridiculously good looking," Mischa replied, noticing that Taylor was still hypnotized by her infatuation. "Come on, we've got to go. Ben's calling the taxi so we can go to the mall instead," she said while tugging on Taylor's sleeve and pulling her away from the tractor beam lock her eyes seemed to have placed on Kai S-Something.

Several hours and several mall cinnamon buns later, Taylor arrived home to the Manhattan Manor. She wasn't positive, but she thought she spotted her parents' car leaving the parking lot. Usually, this would have caused her to panic that something bad had happened, but today she found that she didn't care. After an entire day of skipping school and exploring Kelowna with friends, her negative history with her parents felt as though it was a million years in the past.

◆ ◆ ◆

"They have cars that drive *on* water?" Alexander exclaimed as he and Taylor walked down Bernard Avenue. Even though she knew that her sister had a long day, Vanessa had asked Taylor to take Alexander for a walk that evening, to limit his time in front of the television. Since that evening's dinner was healthy, Taylor decided that they should walk to 7-Eleven to grab Slurpees for dessert.

"Yeah, but they weren't as cool as they sound," Taylor added. She enjoyed how much Alexander liked hearing about her day of skipping school, even if Bedrock City itself was underwhelming. She twisted the straw in her Slurpee around, trying to suck out the melted cream soda flavour syrup that was pooling in the bottom of the cup.

"So, you could drive them on a lake?" Alexander pressed.

"I suppose so," Taylor replied. She hadn't really considered the logistics of bumper boats before. Was it her imagination, or was Alex's face turning pink?

"One day, when I'm old enough, and I have my driver's licence, I'm going to buy a bumper boat," Alexander resolved as he took a long drink from his Slurpee.

"Alex... What flavour did you get?"

"Cream soda, just like you," Alexander responded.

"You're turning pink!" Taylor blurted out.

"Oh, this?" Alexander replied with a grin while holding his hand out. "This is what I told you to remind me to show you! Tara shared a Gatorade with me the other day and I looked like a blueberry! We both had a good laugh." Unsure of how

to respond, Taylor simply smiled as the two of them continued to walk home along the maple-lined street.

Chapter Seventeen

"Are you sure you're not too cool to have your big sis cheer you on at the finish line?" Vanessa asked as she crouched down on the grass where Taylor was double knotting her shoe laces.

"It's only going to be awkward if you make it awkward," Taylor replied with a smile as she stood back up and began to stretch.

"Was that an attempt at sarcasm?" Tara asking jovially as she opened up a plastic cooler that was full of water and sports drinks.

"No, thank you," Mischa said while waving away a bottle of blue Gatorade. "I can't drink anything before I run or I'll feel it sloshing around the entire time."

That day's running event was one of several Milk Runs that the grade eight cross-country running team would have to participate in over the course of the school year. It was a much bigger deal that Taylor had imagined; students from all over the Okanagan region were participating in the event, which was taking place in the Mission neighbourhood of Kelowna. It was an incredibly picturesque area, but this meant that the race would involve lots of hills and obstacles as they would be running alongside orchards.

Taylor looked around at the other runners who were all doing their best to imitate what they imagined real athletes did to prepare for a race: several students were working on their lunges, some jumped around in an attempt to bring up their heart rate, while two awkward boys stood alone eating what appeared to be still-dry instant packs of oatmeal.

Most of the chaperoning parents used their kid's running matches as an excuse to hang back in the parking lot and smoke cigarettes, which made it even more meaningful to Taylor that her sister and Tara were actually going to be cheering at the finish line. Mischa's dad had to work as usual, but since she was pretty much family at this point, Vanessa and Tara wrote her name on their sign too. Mischa claimed that it was embarrassing, but everyone knew she secretly loved the affection.

Taylor was disappointed that Alexander couldn't be there too, but his mail order class work just arrived and he was eager to start learning. Vanessa and Tara agreed that once Alexander learned the basics, they would enroll him in school. Taylor wasn't sure how they would do that without a birth certificate but they told her to stop overthinking and "where there's a will, there's a way." And apparently Vanessa and Tara had both. She wondered if they were going to use the fancy computer that Vanessa had at work, but didn't feel as though she should ask for details.

"So, when do we get this milk we've all been promised?" Taylor asked Mischa, who was also now working on her faux-stretches.

"At the finish line," Mischa replied while doing what could only be described as a clumsy backwards lunge.

"And they have normal, and chocolate?" Taylor pressed, still not fully understanding the concept of a Milk Run. Suddenly, the sound of the referee's whistle screeched across the field and all of the roughly one hundred clumsy teenaged runners made their way to the starting line-up. Both Mischa and Taylor were terrified of getting lost in the crowd, so they had made a pact to run together. They had no trepidation about winning; the only thing that mattered was that they didn't come in last place.

"Good luck, Gagged-On," the snarky voice of Lauren the Ice Queen called out from somewhere behind Taylor.

"Your shoe lace is untied," Taylor replied casually. She hadn't meant it as a rebut to Lauren's insult, it was really just a genuine observation.

"Whatever, loser," Lauren replied with an eyeroll.

Taylor turned back to Mischa; she knew that trying to be Lauren's friend was a lost cause. "You ready?" she asked Mischa, unable to hide the anxiousness in her voice. She had never competed in a race before.

"As long as we can run faster than the two boys eating dried oatmeal, we should be fine," Mischa said with a shrug. One of the boys could be heard wheezing from the back of the crowd, having accidentally inhaled some brown sugar powder.

"EVERYONE, LISTEN UP!" the referee called out. "Just a few ground rules before we get started!"

What is it with teachers and ground rules? Taylor wondered. *This guy sounds just like Mr. Garcia.*

"Make sure you bring a water bottle with you! It's already pretty warm this morning, and we don't want to cart anyone off to the hospital, so stay hydrated! Second rule! No cheating! There will be parents and teachers at all of the potential short-cuts, so don't even try!" An audible groan echoed throughout the crowd.

"Today's race is ten kilometres long, so we're going to give you two hours to complete it before we start looking for strag-glers," the referee continued. "Ribbons for the first, second, and third place runners will be handed out once everyone has made it to the end. And with that, I wish you all good luck!"

Shreeeeeeeeeeeee!

Taylor, and the majority of the other runners, flinched at the loud screech that escaped from the referee's metal whis-tle. After a moment of hesitation, the students all began the race. A handful of kids that were 'too cool' to run, or who had injuries, walked. Taylor and Mischa figured that as long as they maintained a consistent speed walking pace, they would be okay. Heck, maybe they would even place in the top twenty. Sure, other students were pacing them, but Mischa and Taylor would make up for it with endurance!

◆ ◆ ◆

"Tay-lor…" Mischa wheezed from the top of the hill. Or rather, from the top of the slight incline. "I can't keep going. Just, leave me here to die… And please make sure my make-up looks good before they put me in the ground."

"You're being overly dramatic. You ran more than this the other day when we skipped class!" Taylor rarely called Mischa out for being dramatic, but they had been passed by several runners already. While Taylor had never considered herself to be competitive, she realized today that she very much was.

"It's not fair, you're tall! I've got these little legs so I'm basically running twice as far!" Mischa whined.

"I believe in you," Taylor replied earnestly but with a hint of annoyance in her voice, as she grabbed Mischa's hand and began to pull her forward. "Come on, just six kilometres to go! We're nearly halfway."

"Fine, but if I die, I want you to get New Kids on the Block to sing at my funeral."

Taylor nodded, knowing that it wouldn't come to that. Which was a relief for two reasons: she didn't want her only friend to, you know, die. But she also had no idea how she was ever supposed to hire a boy band and couldn't fathom how much money that would take.

"See, this isn't so bad," Taylor offered encouragingly, as they began to make their way back downhill.

"You're right, maybe I can do this after all," Mischa said as she began to catch a second wind.

"Owww…"

"Wait, what's that sound?" Mischa said, coming to a stop once again.

"What sound?" Taylor asked.

"My ankle..."

There it was. Someone was clearly calling out for help, or the wildlife had learned to speak. "Who is that? Are you okay?" Taylor called out while making her way off of the trail and towards a large pine tree, which someone was propped up against. Thanks to the runner's bright hair, Taylor knew who it was before she saw their face.

"Lauren?" Taylor asked. "What happened?"

"What does it look like?" Lauren snapped.

"Come on Taylor, she doesn't want our help," Mischa said while trying to pull Taylor back onto the trail, but Taylor wouldn't budge.

"Meesh, you know we can't leave her here."

"I'll be fine, the chaperones will find me when they do their final walk-through," Lauren said through gritted teeth. Mischa looked around. She wasn't sure if they were miraculously very far ahead, or very far behind everyone. One thing was for certain though, there wasn't another runner around for at least another kilometre or so. A sinking feeling washed over Mischa. She was going to need to be the metaphorically bigger person in this situation and help out her bully. Ugh.

After a moment of hesitation, Mischa crouched down to look at Lauren's ankle. Although she really disliked Lauren, she didn't like to see anyone in pain.

"Don't touch me, dweeb."

"Lauren, can you just… Not be yourself for a little bit?" Mischa said as she rolled down Lauren's knee-high sock and took off her sneaker. "Let me see your ankle. My dad's a nurse so I know a little bit about this stuff." Mischa felt a lump in her throat form as she realized that Lauren's usually tiny ankle was twice the size it should be, and quickly turning a dark purple. It also felt warm to the touch.

"Taylor, you're a giant—" Mischa began.

"Uh, thanks?" Taylor replied, uncertain of where this conversation was going.

"You're going to need to help me stand Lauren up so we can pack her to the finish line," Mischa replied authoritatively.

"I said to just leave me!" Lauren called out. There was something more to her voice. It wasn't just anger. Maybe fear? Taylor wasn't sure.

"Yeah, no. We're not doing that," Mischa argued. "As long as we pack you, and you don't put any weight on your ankle, you'll be fine. We need to get going so you don't go into shock." Mischa wasn't really certain if a broken ankle could put the human body into shock, but she thought it made her sound like she knew what she was talking about.

"Okay, on the count of three," Mischa said while preparing to lift Lauren up so that Taylor could help her walk. "One, two… Three!"

A faint "eep" escaped Lauren's mouth.

"It's okay, we've got you," Taylor said, trying to calm down the former Ice Queen, who was now quite warm to the touch. "Just four kilometres to go, we can do this."

"You guys don't understand… If I don't place in at least the top ten, my dad is going to scream at me," Lauren explained while trying to hold back a woozy feeling that had washed over her. "These shoes were so expensive. My parents, they invest in me, and they expect me to do well in return."

"You got hurt, how could they get mad at you for that?" Mischa asked, realizing that her bully had a human side.

"They get mad at me for a lot," Lauren confessed.

After twenty minutes of awkward silence as Taylor lugged Lauren up and down several hills, the Ice Queen began to defrost. "So… Do you guys know your star signs?" Lauren asked in an uncharacteristically friendly tone. As it turned out, Taylor was a Pieces, and Mischa was a Libra, which to Lauren "totally explained so much!"

As Taylor, Mischa, and Lauren made their way through the remainder of the race course, they were passed by everyone, including the two oatmeal-inhaling boys. Not a single person offered to help either, which Lauren couldn't help but take notice of.

Four kilometres, three snapped walking sticks, an earful of complaints about the pain, and many astrological facts from Lauren later, the three reluctant friends made their way to the finish line. Vanessa and Tara dropped their "Taylor (and Mischa) is are Number 1!" sign and ran towards them at full speed.

They helped to pack Lauren to the nurses' station – a mom who had a first-aid kit in her station wagon – while Taylor and Mischa officially crossed the finish line. The awards ceremony had already begun, which made Taylor realize that no one was ever going to go and look for any stragglers. At least there was plenty of chocolate milk left over.

Chapter Eighteen

As Taylor walked down the empty school hallway, she could hear the clicking sounds of the old oil heaters as they began to turn on for the night. It was late-November now, and the days were getting shorter and colder as winter grew near. While it had only been three months now since she had moved to Kelowna, it was as if a life time had passed since Taylor had left Craigellachie. Yes, class work in a real high school sometimes felt just as repetitive as homeschooled classes, but the monotony was much more enjoyable with friends.

Mischa's birthday party, which she insisted on celebrating late on Halloween was surprisingly uneventful. They were too old to trick or treat, and hadn't been invited anywhere fun, so the two girls and Alexander had stayed up all night eating (or holding) candy while watching spooky movies. They vowed that next year's dual birthday and Halloween celebration would be more memorable. Other day that, the past few weeks had mostly been filled with school work, hanging out at the mall, and helping Alexander with his distanced education classes, and Taylor couldn't have been happier. Life was good.

Taylor felt uncharacteristically proud of herself as she grabbed her binder from her locker; once filled with the unthinkable, the locker was now covered in clippings from Mischa's extensive magazine collection and photobooth pictures of Taylor, Mischa, and Alexander who loved to ham it up for cameras. A smile washed over Taylor's face as she clicked her combination lock shut and made her way to her first after school Events Planning Committee meeting.

The committee was organized by the Student Council, and had actually started back in October. She hadn't planned on signing up, but after some coercion from Lauren, Taylor decided to go for it. In addition to being on several sports teams, Lauren was also the head of the committee and an active Student Council member. Taylor had no idea how she managed to do it all, and truthfully, neither did Lauren. They had both tried to convince Mischa to sign up as well, but Mischa was still a tad frosty towards Lauren after the, well, years of torment. However, she encouraged Taylor to sign up and spread her "little burgeoning social butterfly wings," of course said in Mischa's trademark sarcastic tone. Mischa agreed she would join the committee after Taylor sussed it out and could prove that it wouldn't be a huge train wreck.

While bracing herself with crutches, Lauren managed to wave kindly from the front of the classroom as Taylor took a seat at one of the old wooden desks. A random phone number was carved in it, as well as a few crude sketches that didn't deserve artistic recognition. 'Events Planning Committee' was written in giant swirly letters across the blackboard. "Okay, now that everyone is here, let's begin!" Lauren proclaimed as she kicked off the meeting and hobbled up to the chalkboard. While she was her usual beautiful self, her face was somehow different. It was slightly rounder, and there was a glow about her. It was as if she had overcome something. When asked why she was glowing, Lauren would laugh and say something about good karma. Because high school hierarchies exist in a vacuum, other mean girls began to whisper that maybe Lauren was pregnant. Taylor and Mischa were the only two people that knew the truth: for the first time in many years, Lauren was finally happy.

The meeting was only an hour long, but by the end of it, Taylor was ravenous. A day of classes followed by an hour of event planning was apparently a great way to work up an appetite. Especially with all of the talk about candy grams. Candy grams, to the out of touch, were the primary fundraising method of the Kelowna Secondary School's Student Council. For fifty cents, you could send someone a chocolate bar with a note attached. The intention was for students to send candy to their crushes and friends, but occasionally the candy grams were abused. The council tried to weed out notes that were cruel and bullying, but fifty cents was fifty cents – that money was essential for the committee to pay for the decorations for the school dances.

Because the committee started back in October, most of the planning for the winter dance was already done. It was hotly contested, but the theme was set to be "Under the Sea." Some of the students groaned and whined that it was tacky, but if she was being honest, Taylor had no strong opinion on it. She was just happy to be included. As the newest member of the Events Planning Committee, her responsibilities were pretty small. She would be handing out candy grams next week, and maybe hanging up a few posters. Lauren had also asked her specifically to help plan the Valentine's Day dance after Christmas break, which she was already looking forward to. Maybe she would join Student Council too? Her future felt full of possibilities.

"Meesh, you know I usually trust you but…" Taylor stepped out of her bedroom while wearing a bold coral dress. "I don't know if this is my style."

"Taylor, you look like a million bucks, trust me."

The taffeta dress was knee-length and had poufy shoulders, yet Mischa was convinced that it was going to look incredible on Taylor when they were shopping. When Taylor tried to suggest that Mischa try on this floor-length baby blue gown she spotted, Mischa rolled her eyes and told her that Taylor didn't understand fashion the way she did. She tried the dress on anyway, but Mischa was right, it did look awful on her.

"My first dance, this is unreal," Taylor said to herself, and she and Mischa posed in front of her bedroom mirror. After weeks of planning, it was finally here: The Under the Sea

Dance. Contrasting Taylor's bold ensemble, Mischa was wearing a floor-length solid black gown that she had bought last summer off of a clearance rack. She hemmed it herself and now, as she had said to Taylor moments before, she actually did look like a million bucks. The secondary reason that Mischa liked the dress was that it allowed her to wear insanely tall four-inch-high heels without any of the adults being able to tell, except for the fact that the shoes made her, well, four inches taller.

"You're thirteen dude, how is this your first dance?" Mischa asked.

"I was homeschooled?" Taylor replied, slightly annoyed.

"Yeah, but didn't you like, have a community dance in a barn or something?" Mischa teased. Taylor elbowed her jokingly and the two friends began to laugh.

"Oh my God, look at you two!" Vanessa gushed as she joined Taylor and Mischa in front of the mirror. "You guys are so pretty! Tara! Get the camera!"

"Already on it," Tara replied from the hallway as she loaded a new roll of film into the black Olympus camera.

"How do *I* look?" Alexander asked, also stepping into the increasingly crowded room. He was wearing a black rental suit. Thanks to some of Mischa's ingenuity, Alexander was able to dress up without making the suit soggy. All it took was a little plastic food wrap to line the suit, and some extra foam in the shoes, and presto! Alexander looked ready to host the Kids' Choice Awards. While Alexander wasn't yet a student at K.S.S., the school granted him special permission to attend the dance because Taylor said he was an estranged cousin. She hoped the school would forget her awkward lie by the time Alexander enrolled in the eighth-grade – for real – next fall.

"You all look incredible," Vanessa cooed as Tara prepared to take a group picture.

"Do you think Ben will like the dress?" Mischa asked Taylor, in a rare moment of uncertainty.

"Absolutely. Even Joey McIntyre would dance with you," Taylor replied, proud to have made a successful pop culture reference.

"That is the nicest thing anyone has ever said to me," Mischa replied while brushing her bangs off of her face and looking up in wide-eyed earnestness.

"It's six o'clock, guys! We should get going if you want to make it in time for the dance," Tara called out. Although they lived extremely close to the school, Tara had offered to drive them all there so that they wouldn't mess up their outfits.

"We should probably wait fifteen more minutes," Alexander interjected. "It's important to make a fashionably late entrance."

"He's got a point," Mischa quipped.

As the three friends piled into Big Blue, it began to snow. Alexander stuck his hand out of the window in amazement as a snowflake landed on his palm, but didn't melt. "It's like the sky is raining Slurpees," Alexander observed.

◆ ◆ ◆

After the world's shortest drive, Taylor slammed the truck's heavy passenger door shut and made her way towards the front doors of Kelowna Secondary School. The gentle snowfall was beginning to turn into a full-on snow storm, which made it look as if they were all standing in a very niche snow globe.

"Come on, we're freezing!" Mischa called to Taylor, as Alex shivered in an over-exaggerated way.

"Sorry, let's go in!" Taylor replied as she took a mental picture of her friends. *My first dance, at a real high school, with my best friends. This is so cool.*

The giant school doors swung shut behind them as the friends escaped the snow, swapping the gusty sound of the impending snowstorm for the bassy thuds of the Europop that blared from the school gymnasium.

"Hey guys! I'm glad you're here!" Lauren called from behind the ticket-taking table. Several bunches of baby blue balloons were hanging behind her, presumably to look like bubbles as part of the dance's theme. Her ankle was mostly healed, but the doctor suggested she still keep it easy for a while longer which unfortunately meant she was sitting this dance out. Despite the doctor's orders, Lauren hopped over from behind the desk and greeted everyone with a hug.

"Do you know if Ben's here yet?" Mischa asked.

Lauren returned to the desk and scanned the ticket list. "He is! It looks like he arrived a bit ago."

"Huh, he said he'd meet me out front so we could go in together..."

"Maybe he went to get something from his locker?" Lauren replied, sensing Mischa's unease. After their multi-year rivalry, Lauren didn't want to upset Mischa. "He'll probably show up any minute!"

"Thank you," Mischa replied to both Lauren's words, and intentions.

"Guys, we need to hurry up!" Alexander blurted out while looking up at the nondescript white clock that hung in the school halls. "Our fashionably late entrance is becoming a regular late entrance!"

"Okay, let's go," Taylor said while grabbing both of her friends' hands and leading them into the gymnasium just as the thuds from Technotronic's Pump Up the Jam were replaced with the thuds of Cypress Hill. As the old wooden gym doors swung open, Taylor had a sinking realization: Canadian high school dances were nothing like the movies! While the decorations were fabulous – Taylor had personally helped cut out the green paper streamers that were being used as seaweed – everyone looked just so... Uncool. While in American high school movies everyone would be dancing and, you know, having fun, this dance could hardly be called a dance.

"Why is everyone standing around?" Alexander blurted out, having had the same disappointing realization as Taylor. "This is hardly a dance!"

The three friends stood nervously in the entrance of the gym as Cypress Hill's Insane in the Brain continued to blare from the DJ booth, which was being manned by one of the Audio-Visual Club students. The DJ was wearing sunglasses indoors, which honestly looked pretty great and gave him some credibility, Taylor thought to herself. At least one part of the dance felt cinematic.

"Do either of you see Ben?" Mischa asked, scanning the room of gawkily swaying or just plain-old-standing students. Finally, she spotted him, buying a can of Coke. Mischa made her way through the crowd of students and towards the concession booth.

"Ben, hey! I thought we were going in together?" Mischa called out as sweetly as she could, while also trying to be heard over the music.

Benjamin said something, but Mischa couldn't understand over the music. His face said enough though, as he walked away, leaving her and his can of Coke alone at the concession booth. Mischa felt a sinking in the pit of her stomach. She needed to get out of the gymnasium, immediately.

"Mischa!" Taylor called out as her friend ran past her.

"You don't need him," Taylor said while doing her best to comfort her friend who was currently locked in a bathroom stall.

"He can't dance anyway!" Alexander said, while facing the bathroom wall.

"You can turn around, Alex, no one else is in here," Taylor offered to Alexander.

"Are you sure?" he said while slowly turning around with his eyes still closed.

"Open your eyes," Mischa said to Alexander as she finally left the washroom stall with mascara running down her face.

"Do you want to just go home?" Taylor asked, while Alexander used his spongey hand to wipe the dripping make-up from under Mischa's eyes.

"If I leave now, he wins," Mischa replied with a resolve that both Taylor and Alexander found slightly terrifying.

"Wins what...?" Alexander asked as Mischa walked past the two of them and back towards the gymnasium. This time though, the music that was escaping from the other side of the gymnasium doors was not the bass-filled thuds of hip-hop, but the powerful acapella opening lyrics of Whitney Houston's I Will Always Love You. And then, like a punch to the stomach, she saw it. Right as Mischa returned to the gym, she saw Benjamin approach and then take the hands of some girl from his band class. As the room of teenaged dancers began to awkwardly sway-dance with each other, each keeping the mandated minimum of six inches between them, Mischa felt her tears returning.

"Come on," Alexander said firmly, while grabbing both Mischa's and Taylor's hands and pulling them onto the dance floor. "This dance is nothing like on TV! Let's change that," he said while beginning to move in a strange fashion.

Is he trying to dance? Both of the girls wondered to themselves. Having no sense of rhythm or timing, Alexander's dancing could best be described as flailing, with arguably impressive footwork. Sharing that psychic bond that only teenaged girls seem to have, Taylor and Mischa looked at each other at the same time and shrugged.

With that, the three friends proceeded to ignore the rest of the world and dance their faces off in the middle of the dance floor. To an outsider, it probably looked like they were each having different medical emergencies. The one thing that was apparent to everyone was that they were all doing something that none of the other students were doing: they were actually having fun. The DJ, being the insightful person that he was – after all, he made the smart decision to wear sunglasses to the dance – immediately switched to Whitney Houston's next most popular song, the more fitting I Wanna Dance with Somebody. Without any further instruction needed, the rest of the students joined in and began dancing.

"You're pretty fun," Kai S-Something said as he joined in with the group's odd flail dance. Taylor just smiled.

Chapter Nineteen

Taylor scanned the cafeteria for the cleanest looking empty spot, and aimlessly tossed her bagged lunch onto the table. The background chatter and gossip of the other students merged into a sort of annoying hum that Taylor tried desperately to tune out. Normally she would only get headaches before her 'moon time,' as Lauren called it, much to Mischa's cringe; however today was an exception. All Taylor wanted to do was sleep. She had spent the first two classes of the day nursing a large coffee out of Vanessa's old travel mug, but the caffeine wasn't helping at all.

Although the previous night's school dance ended around 9:00PM, Taylor, Mischa, and Alexander had stayed up giggling and flipping through Mischa's collection of teen magazines until at least 1:00AM. In honour of it being Taylor's very first dance, Vanessa said it was okay for all of them to stay up late. Deep down, Taylor suspected Vanessa of being well aware of how tired they would all be the next day, and used the freedom of an after-midnight bedtime to teach them just how lousy you will feel without a proper eight hours of sleep.

Needless to say, the lesson worked. Just as Taylor debated using her lunch bag as a pillow, she spotted Mischa on the other side of the cafeteria and waved her over.

"Taylor, I don't think I've ever been so tired," Mischa groaned as she brushed crumbs off of an old plastic cafeteria seat and sat down. "I worked retail all summer but this is literally the worst my feet have ever felt. I'm going to burn those high heels when I get home."

"Why don't they have school dances on Fridays so we can all sleep in afterwards?" Taylor asked in earnest.

"Dude, it's so we don't get up to trouble. Kids can only party so hard if they have class the next day," Mischa reasoned.

"Oh hey, it's you guys! High five!" an unknown student said as he approached the two girls, accepted their high fives, and walked away.

"That was odd…" Mischa mumbled.

"You two are real OGs!" another student called out as he carried his lunch tray past Taylor and towards his own table.

"Was that the DJ from last night?" Taylor asked.

"You guys are real party animals! Where's your other friend?" another student called out supportively as they walked by Taylor and Mischa.

"Mischa… I don't want to alarm you but… I think we may be popular?" Taylor wondered, this time with both eyebrows raised.

"Yeah, but at what cost," Mischa replied solemnly as she noticed at least half of the cafeteria was staring at them. "Let's go eat by our lockers." Taylor nodded in agreement as she picked up her lunch bag and made her escape from the zoo which was the K.S.S. cafeteria.

Taylor sighed with relief as she leaned against the wooden door of her locker and slid onto the cool linoleum floor. A few old pieces of paint chipped off of the locker and snagged into Taylor's sweater. The floors had lost their post-summer sheen and were covered in grimy foot prints thanks to the previous night's snow fall, but Taylor didn't care. She just wanted to rest.

"It's not something I had ever considered before but… Taylor, I have a confession," Mischa spoke, wide-eyed.

"What is it?" Taylor said as she opened up her lunch bag and took out her turkey sandwich.

"I really don't want to be popular," Mischa conceded. "And now, I wish I was invisible," she said quietly as Benjamin approached.

"Hey, Meesh, can we talk?" Benjamin asked rhetorically as he took a seat next to Mischa, his typical freshly ironed gingham print shirt looking quite out of place seated in the dirty school hall.

"I mean, you already are," Mischa quipped.

"I just wanted to say, I'm really sorry about how things went last night. I've never had someone openly like me before and I just got scared. I was afraid of disappointing you. Then, after you left, that other girl asked me to dance and I'm not good at saying no, so... That's what you walked in on. It was all a very confusing situation," Benjamin prattled off. "Up until this year, girls just made fun of me. You were the first girl that was nice to me, and I am really sorry that I hurt you."

"I accept your apology," Mischa said softly. Taylor felt like a massive third wheel as she awkwardly ate her sandwich while trying not to eavesdrop.

"Can we just be friends? I really like you, and I want to know you better," Benjamin offered, once again beginning to blush.

"I'd like that," Mischa said. The two of them sat in silence for a moment before Mischa took a granola bar out of her lunch bag and passed it to Benjamin.

"So, who was that awesome guy at the dance with you last night? He seemed to really know how to, uh, bust a move," Benjamin asked once he had consumed half of the granola bar.

"That was my—" Taylor scrambled to think of an answer while swallowing her mouthful of turkey sandwich, "adopted brother, Alexander. He's enrolling in school here next year."

"Well, I can't wait for all of us to hang out," Benjamin said earnestly.

"Me neither," Taylor replied with a smile before looking at her neon pink watch. "I should get going," she said while pushing herself off of the gritty floor and standing up. "I promised Lauren and the rest of the events committee that I would pick up some Christmas bake sale posters from the office and drop them off in the library before next period."

"Are we still going to the mall tonight?" Mischa asked from down on the floor.

"Absolutely," Taylor said with a smile. She may have been exhausted, but Taylor wasn't going to pass up going to the mall on Friday night with friends. She could always sleep in on Saturday.

Chapter Twenty (Epilogue)

That was it, the last box. Taylor looked around at her nearly empty bedroom. Or former bedroom, she reminded herself. The white walls were now entirely empty, save for a few pieces of blue sticky tack that once hung up an assortment of posters. All of her belongings, any sign that she had once lived here, had been packed up into an assortment of boxes. Soon though, she would be able to paint her walls any colour she wanted! Pink was at the top of the list, with purple placing a close second. Since Vanessa and Tara had finally saved enough to buy a house of their own, they had promised Taylor and Alexander that they would each get to paint their bedrooms any colour they wanted. The house was only a few blocks away, just off of Bernard Avenue, which also meant Mischa could still pop by anytime she wanted.

Having just completed eighth grade, it was hard to believe it had already been nearly a year since Taylor had moved from Craigellachie to Kelowna. Not many thirteen-year-old girls had the guts to strike out on their own the way that Taylor had done, but man was it worth it. While she didn't feel brave in the moment, after completing a year in a real school and making genuine friends, Taylor felt like she could now take on the world. Her life in the no-place of Craigellachie felt like it was in the distant past.

"If you stand around here all day, Alex is going to beat you picking out the best room in the new house," Vanessa said jokingly as she walked up behind Taylor and messed up her hair. Vanessa didn't need to mention that Alexander was also incredibly impatient to bring his Grow a Friend puppy to life. He had been counting down the hours until they moved into the new house for the last month. There wasn't room in the apartment, but the new house would have plenty of room for the damp little puppy paws.

"Just taking one last look around," Taylor replied calmly.

"Sounds good, Stringbean. I'll give you some space. When you're ready you and Alex can help Tara load the last few boxes into Big Blue," Vanessa said as she gently closed the door to Taylor's old bedroom.

Taylor looked at the floor where her old nightstand once sat. She looked over at where she had discovered Alexander on the floor and nearly had a heart attack. It was sad to her that the Grow a Friend toys were pulled from store shelves before they were set to be released for Christmas. Taylor didn't have the details, but she was grateful to have Alex in her life and to know that he had escaped the massive emergency Grow a Friend recall. While the media was mostly silent on the matter, Taylor had a hunch that more information would come out about this down the road.

She thought back to all of the times that her and Mischa had gotten ready for school in the morning in this very room. While she was feeling nostalgic, this was a happy day. When she moved from her parents' house, Taylor imagined that she would be moving into just another place: she didn't know she would be moving into a real *home*. Just like a fish in a bowl, Taylor had once again outgrown her space, but this time, she found a family to grow with her.

As Taylor left the Manhattan Manor for the last time and hopped into Tara's extremely cramped Ford Ranger next to the spongey Alexander, she had the realization that sometimes things aren't like on TV, and that's okay. In fact, it's better.

ACKNOWLEDGEMENTS

A big and sappy heartfelt thank you to the following:

Chorong Kim, for designing another gorgeous cover and helping to bring my characters to life;

Pip Wallace, for proofreading and drastically improving this book;

Graeme Good, for always believing in me and being supportive when I have my *artist moments,* and for editing assistance;

and Tanya Gust, Becca Shaw, and Lucy Bannard, for providing so much feedback along the way and for always encouraging me to keep going!

I would also like to thank Donna Markin & Ron Stevenson of Primaris Management Inc., Cyndi Ramsfield, Dayna Culham, and Trina Manca of School District 23, and Wendy Kwok and the team at the BC Dairy Association, for their assistance with historical research.

Ashley Good is an author and independent filmmaker from British Columbia, Canada.

While she grew up in the almost-place of Sicamous, Ashley now calls Vancouver Island home.

You can check out more of her work at ashleygood.ca.